W9-BWW-510

A Lova' Like No Otha'

Stephanie Perry Moore

WARNER BOOKS

An AOL Time Warner Company

Walk Worthy Press

West Bloomfield, Michigan

All Scripture references are from the King James Version of the Bible, copyright © 1985, Holman Bible Publishers.

Copyright © 2003 Stephanie Perry Moore

Reading Group Guide copyright 2003 by Warner Books, Inc., with Walk Worthy Press.

Published by Warner Books, Inc., with Walk Worthy Press

Real Believers, Real Life, Real Answers in the Living God™
Walk Worthy Press, 33290 West Fourteen Mile Road, #482, West Bloomfield, MI 48322

Warner Books, Inc., 1271 Avenue of the Americas, New York, NY 10020

An AOL Time Warner Company

Printed in the United States of America

First Printing: June 2003

ISBN 0-7394-3505-1

In memory of my dear uncle
HECTOR ROUNDTREE
(1957–2000).

Though the storm of cancer kept raging in your life, you are now through it and resting in the arms of the Lord.

It's my fondest hope that everyone who reads this book will understand that they too can get through any storm as long as Jesus Christ is captain of their ship.

Thanks for saying you were proud of me. One day in heaven, I'll tell you how much that meant as we praise the Greatest Love of all!

Acknowledgments

Boy, did I long to feel hugs, kisses, and a whole lot more from my husband, but today that wasn't happening. He's out of town with his new job and though I'm certain he'd be happy to oblige me . . . duty calls at work. I should be able to understand, right? Wrong! I want to be loved. Mad, angry and bitter, I pouted most of the day. Till God whispered gently in my ear, "Can I love you today?" Of course the answer was yes. And when I let go my fleshly desires and clung to His Spirit, then and only then was I whole and satisfied.

For anyone who longs to be filled with people, places and things, this novel is for you.

For my parents, Dr. and Mrs. Franklin D. Perry Sr., I love the way you raised me. I am who I am because of it.

For Denise Stinson, I love the way you believed in me. I have this chance to touch many lives through print because of that chance.

For my assistants, Nakia Austin, Andrea Johnson and Nicole Duncan, I love your work ethics. I finished this novel because I could depend on you.

For my interns, Jamie McNair and Shayla Turner, I love how much you admired my writing. My time with you gave me a chance to do more, care more, and give more to my readers.

For Kathy Ide and Victoria Christopher Murray, I love how you helped me. Your determination to make this project the best it could be touched my heart.

For my extended family, Rev. and Mrs. Dewey E. Perry Sr., Viola Roundtree, Ann Redding, Dennis, Leslie, little Franklin, the

Bates family, the Perry family, the Moore family, the Roundtree family, the Hayes family, the Randall family, the Williams family and the Manning family, I love the support you give to my life. Your always being there helps me soar high.

For Warner/Walk Worthy authors and staff, especially my editor, Frances Jalet-Miller, I love working with you. Being a part of such a great organization is a great joy.

For my dear friend, Chandra "Jackie" Dixon, I love our relationship. Your laughs keep me going.

For my former NFL wives crew, Laundria Perriman, Gloria London, Torian Colon, Robin Swilling, Kim Porcher, Kathleen Hanson, Laura Kasay, Sherrie Rodenhauser, Linda Reich, Tracy Williams, Nicole Smith, Tracy Sanders, and so many others, I love the times we shared. Those moments are embedded in my heart forever.

For my sorority sisters in Delta Sigma Theta, especially the Delta authors, I love our bond. The support you all have shown me is proof that we do support our own.

For my daughters, Sydni and Sheldyn, I love being your mommy. Thanks for being real proud of me and telling all your friends that mom is a "Book Sign."

For my husband, Derrick, I love you. You fill my soul with heat and passion, and boy do I love that feeling.

For the reader, I love that you gave this book a chance. I pray that your walk with the Lord is strengthened.

For my Lord and Savior, Jesus Christ, I love how much You love me. Thanks for showing me why all I need is Your love.

Chapter 1

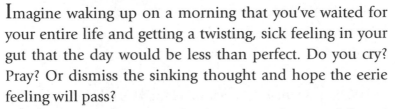

Imagine waking up on a morning that you've waited for your entire life and getting a twisting, sick feeling in your gut that the day would be less than perfect. Do you cry? Pray? Or dismiss the sinking thought and hope the eerie feeling will pass?

I chose the latter. On the morning of my wedding, I woke up to the sound of thunder. The rain outside my hotel room was so thick, I couldn't see two feet outside my window.

While in college, I had met my fiancé, Devyn Jackson, at a school picnic in Tri-City Park. A couple of years later, he proposed to me there, so it seemed perfect for us to get married in that enchanting location. But now my plans for an outdoor wedding were being washed away.

Still, I was determined not to let this storm ruin the most important day of my life. I had prepared a backup plan, so things weren't totally destroyed. Besides, I didn't have time to fret.

Picking up my emergency list, I made the first phone call.

"Pastor Porcher, this is Zoe."

"Good morning." His voice boomed through the receiver. "How are you on this blessed day?"

My eyes roamed to the window, where the raindrops pelted the glass. "Not too good, Pastor. It looks like my wedding is a washout."

"Oh, no, child. Rain is just a cleansing from the Lord. This is still a beautiful day because this is a day that the Lord has made."

It was good to hear that the pastor thought the rain was God's cleansing. I was thinking that maybe the Lord was crying, kind of like the overwhelming sadness parents feel when they think their child is making a mistake. However, I had prayed too many times for God to be all up in my plans.

"Well, I do have a backup plan." I took a long, deep breath.

After telling the pastor about the wedding changes, I actually felt a bit better. Pastor Porcher was so close to my family. Next I phoned the wedding planner. She agreed to handle calling the caterer, band and florist.

I took a deep breath before I called my best friend and maid of honor, Tasha. Though she was my girl, our relationship was weird. I loved her but wasn't 100 percent sure she felt the same way.

"Hey, girl," I said in the cheeriest voice I could muster. "Just wanted to make sure you were up."

"You don't have to check on me." Tasha yawned. I could almost see her stretching before she said, "Hey, it's raining out there."

"I know," I moaned. "But I'm getting everything together for Plan B. I should be on my way to the church in ten minutes."

"Sorry you can't have your outdoor wedding. Girl, I just hope this ain't a sign that your marriage is doomed." She chuckled. When I didn't say anything, she quickly added, "Just joking."

"Don't play with me, Tasha," I said, my voice shaking. "This day is going to be stressful enough. Please don't be late."

"Don't worry. I'll be at the church before you get there, even if I have to run every red light. It'll be cool; you'll see."

I hung up the telephone a moment before my mother, Marzella, walked in from her adjoining room. My fifty-year-old mother looked as if she hadn't slept. People often told her that she didn't look her age. She was always told she looked younger. She didn't look her age today either. . . . She looked ten years older. She seemed so tired and worn out.

"Don't worry, honey. Your day will be perfect," Mom said, "even with the rain."

Why did everyone have to focus on the rain? I wondered as she hugged me. My mother and I didn't talk much, but I never had any doubt that she loved me. She just never understood my needs. Also, after my father died, she'd done things that I still held against her and that kept a distance between us.

When the phone rang, my mother smiled and waved. "See you at the church."

My hand motioned back to her. Then she took a few seconds to gather stuff. When I was finally alone, I answered the phone.

"Hey, baby. It took you so long to answer. You ain't got no man up in there, do you?" Devyn said, slurring his words. "What time am I supposed to, umm, marry you?"

I sighed. "Devyn, are you drunk?"

I don't know why I asked the question. The night before, Devyn's groomsmen had given him a bachelor party. A couple of my girlfriends spied on them because their husbands were there. As I half listened to Devyn deny that he was drunk, I recalled the middle-of-the-night phone call I'd received.

It was after three when the phone rang, and I answered on the first ring.

"Girl, you're not going to believe what's going on at that party," Breann screamed through the phone without saying hello.

"Yeah, girl," Jessica piped in. "It's wild. They have women. . . ."

"I don't want to hear this," I told them as I sat up in the bed. I turned on the light. "I don't need to know what my future husband is doing. After tomorrow, we'll be married and none of this will matter."

I hung up, turned off the light and spent the rest of the night resting in peace.

But I found no peace in the morning. First the storm, now Devyn calling drunk. I shuddered at the thought of what really happened at his party.

"Okay, baby. Maybe I had a few drinks," Devyn finally admitted. "But I'm not drunk. Really," he slurred.

I rolled my eyes. "Devyn, you need to drink some coffee—extra black. Be at the church by two."

"I'll be fine, baby. I promise."

I looked at the clock. There were still three hours before the ceremony, but I wanted to get to the church as soon as I could. As I stood and began to gather my things, I thought about our courtship.

Devyn and I met when we were students at the University of Miami. He was a senior and I was a junior. I first noticed him during my freshman year, but he was quite popular with the ladies and too involved with football to notice me. The light-skinned Shemar Moore look-alike had it going on.

During my junior year, I became an official hostess for the football team. My main responsibility was to introduce high-school athletes—prospective candidates—to our school. Throughout the year, the hostesses participated in activities with the football players. Our first event that year was a welcome picnic in a park near the campus for the hostesses and the players.

I remembered that Saturday, four years before, as if it were yesterday. Most of the people at the picnic knew each other. The majority of the girls had been hostesses the previous year. I didn't know many people, but that didn't matter. Devyn Jackson was my favorite football player, and he was the only one I wanted to meet. Since my earliest freshman day, I had followed his career. I knew all of his statistics. He was one of the top cornerbacks in the country. "Interception Man" was his nickname. Observing Superman, people would always say, "Up, up, and away!" Well, for Devyn, on game days, the crowd always screamed, "Take, take it away!"

I figured the picnic would be the perfect opportunity to meet this awesome guy. So I mixed and mingled, chatting with all the ball players . . . except Devyn. After a few hours, he still had not made an appearance. Apparently he was going to ruin our chance meeting by not showing up.

Frustration flooded through my body like water. To get my mind off my fantasy guy, I chilled. I started stuffing my face with ribs and potato salad.

I can't believe this, I thought, unable to shake that fine black man I'd only seen in passing. *This picnic is the only chance I have to meet him. Oh, well.* I sighed. *Nothing I can do about it.*

"Excuse me." A deep, husky voice above me interrupted my conversation with myself. "Is somebody sittin' here?"

"No," I said, waving my hand in a carefree motion, not even looking up to see who was asking. I returned to gnawing on my barbecued ribs.

"So, is the food that good?" the voice asked, this time from beside me.

My honey brown five-foot five-inch body, with a cute layered hairdo, turned and said, "Yeah, real good." I could feel the barbecue sauce dripping from the edge of my lips. I almost fainted. I was staring into the eyes of the man whom I wanted to meet.

Devyn Jackson grinned, picked up a napkin and, with the corner, gently wiped the sauce from my mouth. From that moment on, that good-looking, light-skinned brotha' was all I wanted.

I drove to the church as the rain flooded the streets. My windshield wipers thumped an insistent rhythm, barely keeping my view clear enough to navigate. Although most of my plans were ruined, I was still happy about the wedding. I was marrying the love of my life and looking forward to our future.

But the moment I tried to imagine our wedding night, a brilliant flash of lightning crackled across the sky, followed by a violent thunderclap. My body shook. The fears I had been keeping so carefully tucked away seemed to surface all at once.

"God," I groaned. "I know Devyn isn't where he needs to be in his faith, but he'll grow," I promised the Lord. "Devyn and I have been through many storms, and You've seen us through every one." I thought about all the partying, drinking and fornicating we'd done. "I know I've disappointed You by compromising in certain areas with Devyn. I know I am not bringing virginal purity to my wedding; maybe my white dress is a lie. But even through my disobedience, You were always there when I called."

The tears from my eyes began to match the downpour that came from the heavens. It was more than thinking about the things I'd done with Devyn. I never thought he would ask me to be his bride. Most of the time when we discussed marriage, he said he wasn't ready.

Overcome with emotion, I maneuvered my car alongside a curb, my tires interrupting a river of rainwater. I wanted to talk to the Lord freely, without distractions. I turned off the engine, humbly bowed my head and closed my eyes.

"Thank you for changing Devyn's mind, Lord," I continued. "And for putting so many things together for us. Through the planning for this wedding, even my mother and I have grown closer. I love You, Jesus! And although Devyn isn't a strong believer yet, I know that through my life influence he'll be one soon."

My body wouldn't move. It just stayed in that position, thinking and talking to the Lord. I wasn't sure how much time had passed before I finally said, "Amen." I really wanted to spend more time with God, but I knew I had to get to the church.

Lifting my head, I was surprised to see that the downpour had ended, leaving behind only sprinkles. By the time I arrived at the church ten minutes later, the sun was peeking from behind the thick clouds.

"Maybe I can have the wedding outside after all," I said as I jumped from the car. I opened the trunk and began unpacking the suitcases and boxes I'd brought with me. But just as I gathered the last load from the car, the rain started again.

It wasn't going to bother me, though. Plan B was already in motion. I rushed to the dressing room, holding my enormous gown across my arms and carrying two plastic bags filled with my shoes, panty hose, hair spray, makeup and jewelry. Passing the sanctuary, I glanced through the doors and had to stop at the sight. The room was decorated beautifully, with sky blue flowers and ribbons and lace everywhere! I wanted to stand and admire it, but I knew there wasn't time.

When I got to the dressing room, all seven of my attendants were there, dressed in the baby blue bridesmaid gowns I'd selected. In their full-length satin dresses, my friends were all that.

"You guys are the bomb," I said as my girls took the packages from my arms. "Thanks for helping my mother decorate the church. I know it was last minute, but everything is beautiful."

"Zoe, where have you been?" Tasha asked, her hands on her hips. "You said you'd be here an hour ago."

I thought about the time I'd spent with God but remained silent.

"The wedding is gonna start soon," Tasha continued to rave. "You gotta hurry and get dressed, girl."

"I will. Everything will be fine. I needed a little time alone with me and God." I paused. "I just want to say that I appreciate all of you." I stopped again, letting my eyes roam to each of my friends. "Thank you for sharing in my special day." I swallowed, clearing the lump in my throat. "Oh, help me put on my gown before I get all emotional!"

My friends chuckled, though I could see in their eyes their strong emotions too. But we got to work. I slipped from my jeans and shirt, slid into the underwear that was designed for my dress and finally stepped into my gown.

Within thirty minutes from when we started, I was completely dressed, staring at myself in the mirror.

"Oh, you look beautiful," Tasha gushed as my mother pushed me into the chair so that she could do my makeup. By the time I looked in the mirror again, I looked like a blushing bride, eagerly awaiting the man I loved.

"It's time," my mother said as she leaned over and kissed me on the cheek. "I'll see you in the sanctuary."

I nodded because I didn't want to cry and watched as my bridesmaids lifted their white lily bouquets one by one and lined up outside the room for the processional.

Finally, when only Tasha was left, she handed me my larger bouquet. I stood and she adjusted my four-foot train. Then she looked at me with misty eyes. "This is it, girl," she said, giving me a trembling smile.

Tasha took my hand and we joined the bridesmaids in the hall. But a moment later, Brandi, one of my hostesses, rushed past the bridesmaids, making her way to me.

"Zoe!" Her face seemed as white as my bridal gown.

"Are they ready for us?" Tasha asked.

"Almost," Brandi replied, breathing as if she'd just run a marathon. She paused to catch her breath. "But that's not why I came over." She lowered her voice so the bridesmaids couldn't hear. "Girl, can we go back into the dressing room for a minute? We need to talk."

"Now?" I couldn't imagine what she had to say that couldn't wait until after the ceremony.

"Now," Brandi insisted, giving me the eye that something wasn't right.

Tasha and I looked at each other; then she grabbed the train of my gown and moved it so I could retrace my steps.

Back inside the dressing room, Brandi closed the door. I wanted to sit down, but I didn't dare wrinkle my dress. "Well?" I asked, holding up my hands impatiently. "What's so important? Is my slip showing? Do I have food in my teeth? What?"

"I thought you should know," Brandi said, her fingers intertwined so tightly the knuckles went white. "I saw Devyn kissing another girl."

My pulse instantly started racing, but I tried to calm myself, keeping my breaths even. "Well," I responded, as if I weren't a bit concerned, "he was probably saying good-bye to an old flame. You know what a big flirt Devyn is. Was," I said, correcting myself.

"It wasn't a peck," Brandi said. "It was a serious kiss. And there's more. After they let up, he and the girl walked back into his dressing room with their arms wrapped around each other. I stuck around, keeping my eye on the door and praying there was nothing really going on. But, Zoe, they were in there for a long time. And when they came out, Devyn wasn't wearing his tuxedo anymore."

"You don't know what you're talking about," I exclaimed, unable to come up with a better response. I glanced at Tasha, who just stared silently and wide-eyed at Brandi.

"Oh, yeah?" Brandi retorted. I could tell that my friend was annoyed that I didn't believe her. She continued: "Well, when Devyn came out, dressed in his regular clothes, and that girl followed him, I knew something was up. And when they started talking to the pastor and Devyn's best man, I figured that I'd better tell you." She paused, then added, "I thought you'd want to know."

I couldn't speak around the lump in my throat. I shook my head, attempting to clear my mind. "There's no way Devyn would do what you're saying. It can't be true."

But my words had barely left my lips when I heard a

knock on the door. Tasha looked at me, silently asking if I wanted her to answer it. She didn't always have my back, but I knew she did then. So I nodded.

The door opened and there stood my groom, wearing jeans and an unironed brown T-shirt. And holding some chick's hand. She had a waterfall hairstyle that was tinted blue, and she wore a small gold nose ring. Her extra-long acrylic fingernails were painted in myriad colors and designs. One of her front teeth was capped in gold. What a joke.

Tasha was the first to move. She walked over to Devyn. "Who is this?" she asked, flicking her hand in the girl's face.

Devyn glared at my maid of honor. "Tasha, like always, you've got your nose stuck in other people's business. Please leave so I can talk to Zoe in private. You too, Brandi."

Tasha and Brandi looked at me. I shrugged, letting them know that it was okay. But I knew that they would be standing right outside the room, waiting for the first chance to jump on Devyn if I called.

Tasha and Brandi slowly sauntered toward the door. As they passed Devyn, they rolled their eyes.

He stepped inside the room, the tacky girl still clutching his hand. A moment later, he whispered in her ear. From the way her eyes shifted, I could tell that she didn't agree with what Devyn was saying. Finally, she turned and left the room. But not before she sized me up and laughed.

Devyn closed the door and walked toward me.

"Dev-yn," I began, trying not to sound too whiny. I didn't want to. But I couldn't help it. "Our wedding is going to begin at any moment. Why aren't you dressed? And who's that girl?"

He gently grasped my arm and led me to the chair where I had sat minutes before getting my makeup done so that I could look beautiful for the man I loved. "Sit down, Zoe. Please," he said softly.

I was no longer concerned about getting wrinkles in my dress. I was too frightened to care. I nervously plopped down. "We really don't have time for this, Devyn. Our guests are waiting. We're getting married in a little while."

He bit his lower lip and stared at a corner of the floor. "I am getting married, Zoe. Just not to you. I'm so sorry."

"What?" I exclaimed, my breath coming in gulps.

"That woman with me—her name is Aisha. I've known her for a little over a year, ever since I got that job as bank manager in Tampa Bay. We work together. She's a teller."

I stared at Devyn as if he were speaking a foreign language.

"About eight months ago, we started going out to lunch together, staying late after work a few times. And . . . well . . ."

"What are you saying?"

He walked to the other side of the room, turning away from me. "Aisha told me a few minutes ago that she's pregnant . . . with my child."

All the blood drained from my face. I wondered if there was a paper bag in the room, in case I needed to breathe into it to keep from passing out. This couldn't be happening.

"I love you, Zoe." Devyn's voice cut into the haze in my mind. "But I love her too. I thought I wanted to spend the rest of my life with you. But when Aisha told me about the baby . . . things changed."

I stared at his back. Even with all that he was telling me, he still wouldn't face me. He couldn't look into my eyes and tell me this mess.

Before I knew what I was doing, I stood and flew over to him. When he turned around, I slapped him hard across his cheek. The sound of my palm's meeting his flesh echoed throughout the small room. "You bastard!" I hollered. "How could you do this to me?"

I screamed and punched him in the chest, moving my arms like a wild animal. He didn't budge. Devyn never raised his hands. He just stood there, taking my blows.

Moments later, the door swung open and Tasha burst into the room with Devyn's best man and roommate, Chase Farr, right behind her. It took the two of them to pull me away from Devyn, moving me back to my makeup chair.

"Come on, girl," Tasha said, kneeling before me and still holding my hands. "You don't want to go out like that."

Though tears still filled my eyes and my heart, I nodded and took deep breaths.

"That's the way to do it." Tasha's voice was soothing.

I glanced over at the corner where Devyn stood with Chase, whispering and looking at me like I needed to be committed to some mental institution. But I kept breathing deeply, wanting to calm myself.

I heard someone step into the room, and turned to the door. Aisha stood as if she belonged there. Then she walked slowly toward Devyn.

I broke from Tasha to cut her off. The long train of my gown slowed me down—but only a little.

"What kind of a girl would come to another woman's wedding and steal her groom?" I yelled.

The girl tried to walk around me, ignoring me and my question. I grabbed her arm and raised my fist, knowing I could take her if it came to that. Though she looked ghetto, I too was from the streets.

"Don't you hear me talkin' to you?"

Chase grabbed me around the waist and led me away. At 6 feet and 200 pounds, he easily pulled my 5-foot 5-inch, 115-pound frame into a corner, turning me away from Devyn and Aisha.

"Come on, Zoe. You have too much class for this," he mumbled into my ear.

When I looked up into Chase's sincere eyes, I saw his tears that matched my own.

Chase had been Devyn's roommate at the University of Miami, where he was a star football player too. I knew he always liked me. I could tell by the way he stared at me when he thought I wasn't looking, or by the way he spoke to me—in a gentle, loving tone. He was always there to console me every time I caught my man cheating. But he never pursued me because he knew I was in love with his best friend, no matter what Devyn did. Although Chase often told me I could do better than Devyn, I guess I never believed him until now.

"What's going on?" a new voice asked. I turned toward the door and saw my brother, Alonzo, standing with my mother beside him. Alonzo was supposed to be giving me away since our father was deceased. He had been looking forward to the wedding almost as much as I had.

I turned back, looking deep into Chase's dark eyes. "I can't handle this. I've got to get out of here."

"I'll go with you."

I took two steps toward the door, then stopped. "I can't leave. All my friends and family are here."

Tasha touched my arm. "Don't worry about anything here. I'll handle it. Just go with Chase. Everything will be fine." She lifted my purse from the table and gave it to me.

I hugged her, then rushed past my mother and brother and the other bridesmaids, who were still lined up in the hallway, now whispering about what was going on. I fled through the church doors, with Chase right behind me.

The day was exactly the way it'd been this morning—dark, gray and ugly. My elegant wedding dress collected a layer of mud along the hem as I trudged to my Ford Probe.

Getting into my car would have been hysterical to watch if I hadn't been so . . . well, hysterical. The crown of my veil caught on the top of the doorway, yanking out the carefully placed bobby pins, which in turn pulled out several strands of hair. I winced, then hollered and grabbed my veil, pushing it back onto my head. It sat crookedly and part of the white mesh draped over my left eye. I plopped into the driver's seat, but most of my dress remained outside the car.

"Zoe, wait. Let me help you." Chase tried to stuff in as many layers of the satin dress as he could before I grabbed the handle and slammed the car door shut, catching the muddy hem in the frame.

Chase hurried around to the other side of the car while I dug through my purse for the keys.

"Ouch!" I exclaimed. The veil pulled my hair again now that it was wedged between my back and the car seat. Finally, my frantic search produced keys and I started the engine.

Just as I got the car started, Devyn ran up and pounded on my window. I glared at him through the glass. He looked like a fool standing in the rain, his naturally curly hair drenched and flat. Then I wondered, who looked like the bigger fool—him or me?

"I don't have anything to say to you," I yelled, jamming the gear into drive.

Devyn flew to the front of the car and planted his hands on the hood. I revved the engine with my right foot, keeping my left foot pressed hard against the brake.

"Hold up," Chase yelled. "You can't run him over. I'll talk to him."

I returned the car to park, then took my foot off the gas pedal. Chase jumped from the car. I watched the two, standing and being pelted by the rain, as Chase tried to talk to Devyn.

I rolled down my window, just enough. "I just wanted to apologize," I heard Devyn say, "and tell her I never meant to hurt her."

"You've said enough already," Chase replied. "You've been pulling this junk on her for years. Dev, she's finally had enough. Now, leave her alone."

"But—"

"Let her go, man."

As they continued, I lowered my eyes and turned inward. I felt empty—there was nothing inside me. I'd lost it all—everything that was important to me.

Without thinking, I put the car into drive again and inched forward. It made the men stop talking and they stared at me, their eyes wide. In the next second, they both jumped out of my way and I screeched off, leaving them both behind.

The rain had turned the streets into rivers. So once I turned on two wheels from the church's parking lot, I slowed down, maintaining that steady pace. I drove, with no destination in mind. I aimlessly roamed the streets. But twenty minutes later, I found myself at the park—where my perfect outdoor wedding was to have taken place.

After pulling into a parking space in the empty lot, I reached behind and ripped off my veil. Then I grabbed the tape player and cassette box off the seat and opened the door. My enormous dress billowed out of the car as if it were grateful to be free. With my veil in one hand and the tape player and cassette box in the other, I stomped toward the gazebo, not caring that my dirty, tattered dress would now also be wet.

I stood right outside the redwood circle. Even with the wind and the rain, a few white crepe paper streamers still clung to the roof of the gazebo, like they were holding on to a memory. This was all that was left of the decorations that my friends and I had excitedly put up the previous night when there wasn't the slightest hint of any storm.

For several moments, I stood, with the rain beating down on me, staring at the banner still hanging across the archway. It screamed CONGRATULATIONS! in blue letters out-lined in gold.

"Congratulations," I muttered. "That's a joke."

I tripped up the three steps and then plunked down on a wet bench inside the gazebo. My dress was now drenched with tears and rain. I stared at what was left of my veil before I tossed it into a nearby hedge. I opened the cassette box and pulled out my Yolanda Adams tapes. I searched the covers and saw what I was looking for—the album *Through the Storm.*

I inserted the cassette into the tape player, ignoring the wind that had kicked up and the hail that had started to fall. But when the gazebo walls began to rock from strong gusts, I grabbed the tape player and cassette box and dashed back to my car.

Stuffing my dress into the driver's seat was even more difficult now that it was wet and muddy.

Sitting inside my Probe, I wondered where I could go. The church was out of the question because guests might still be there—or even worse, Devyn might be hanging around, waiting to see if I returned. I couldn't go to my mother's apartment in the projects because it was so small and I knew I wouldn't have privacy. The reception was sup-posed to be there, and you know black folks—even though the wedding was off, I'm sure people were planning to go over there and get some free food. And I was sure that my friends and family had probably gathered there to discuss my humiliation.

So, I sat with the hail beating its rhythm on the roof and hood of my car. For a moment, a thought played through my mind. I could go to Orlando. Devyn had booked a honeymoon suite at Disney World. It seemed only fair that someone should enjoy it. And that someone could be me.

I pushed the play button on the car's cassette deck. The hail was beginning to let up as I listened to Yolanda sing about the storms of life. I compared the weather outside to the blow I'd just received from my fiancé.

After a moment, I noticed that the beat of the song matched the slap of the windshield wipers. But both sounds were drowned out by my sobs.

"Lord," I prayed, "I don't understand why You didn't give me the desire of my heart. I know You want what's best for me. But right now, this sure hurts!"

In addition to the hurt, I was afraid. I couldn't imagine what tomorrow would hold for me. I had quit my job at the Marriott as a hotel management trainee; I had talked my way out of my apartment lease; I had donated most of my belongings to charity the weekend before. All to be with Devyn. Now I had no husband, no job, no money and no home. Everything I owned—other than the stained, ragged wedding gown clinging to my damp skin—was in the two suitcases in the trunk of my Probe.

I let my tears flow, though I carefully maneuvered through the rain outside, still not really knowing where I was headed. But after only a few minutes, I could feel the presence of God. I knew that Jesus was holding me in His arms. I knew that no matter how much I hurt, God would heal this wound. Just like He'd healed all my other ones.

There were so many times that God had rescued me. I remembered when my father passed away. I was a sad little five-year-old girl sitting on the floor by his favorite chair, just hoping he'd walk back through the door and sit in it. He always sat in that old dusty chair. And when he was comfortable, he reached for me and let me sit in his lap till I fell asleep.

I wasn't the only one who was sad. My mother had cried for two weeks straight. Her tears could have made a garden grow. She loved my daddy. Though I was young, I knew it. They hugged all the time.

She was angry with him, though, about a month after he was gone. She cried, "Why'd you have to go to the store in that storm? I told you I didn't need any wine. Dang it! You would still be here if you had just listened. Now you're gone and we have no money. I hate you. . . . I hate you." My brother calmed her down and later she apologized to my dad at his grave. Yep, I had no doubt she loved him. Sadly, though, he'd be the only man she'd ever love. Or maybe though it was brief, at least she felt deep love once in her life.

I didn't know how I'd go on after my dad's death. I was sure I'd never be happy again. But God stepped in and worked everything out. Within weeks, I began to feel better and healed more every day, so I knew I'd be okay this time too. I was standing on His promise that He's the same God yesterday, today and forever.

I recited what I believed in my mind. I believed that God could do anything except fail. I believed that He would bring me the right man, the right job, the family I longed for. He would do all these things and more. I just had to be patient and understand His timing.

The Scriptures where Jesus had calmed a storm at sea when He was with His disciples came to my mind. He had uttered simple words: "Peace; be still." I needed that miracle of peace to calm my storm.

By the time Yolanda's song ended, I was beginning to feel a part of the peace that I wanted. It was then that I decided not to go to Orlando. It didn't make sense to run to another city for comfort when I needed to run to Jesus. It was His serenity that I craved. Calmly, I drove back to the church.

My eyes widened with surprise when I drove into the church's parking lot. It was still packed with cars. I had suspected that some people would still be here, but not this many.

I took a few deep breaths and then bravely got out of my car. I slowly walked up the steps, then inside toward the sanctuary. I stood at the wide doors, staring at my family and friends. They were hovering near the front, whispering. I could imagine their words of pity. My soiled wedding gown dripped water, forming a puddle on the carpet beneath me.

Tasha turned and saw me first. "Zoe!" she called out.

Everyone followed her gaze. There was a moment of stunned silence before they rushed to me, crowding around. My mother located a blanket, placed it around my shivering shoulders, then led me to a pew where I could sit down before my quivering knees gave way.

I could feel some of the peace that I asked God for, in the midst of my friends. I was surrounded by people who loved me, and I was glad I hadn't gone off to Orlando by myself.

"Is she okay?" I heard someone ask.

"I'll be fine," I answered for myself. "What Devyn did was terrible. But you know what? It's better that he walked out today than after we got married."

I paused. Heads nodded, while other people mumbled their agreement.

"Sure, things look bad right now," I continued. "But I know my Lord will provide a way out of this. You see, Jesus and I aren't staying in the dark."

The muttering of agreement got louder. For a moment, I thought my friends and family were going to cheer.

Feeling momentum, I stood up and repeated what I'd just said. "Jesus and I aren't staying in this darkness. We're just walking through some frightening thunder!"

Chapter 2

My brother brought one of my suitcases to me.

"Let me help you change," Tasha said, and my mother nodded.

"No, I'm fine. I'll be out in a few minutes."

I ducked into the rest room and slipped out of my ruined wedding gown into jeans and a sweater. When I looked in the mirror, I couldn't believe what I saw. My face was streaked with mascara, my eyes were swollen from my tears and my hair was a tangled mess. I washed my face, brushed my hair, then went back into the sanctuary, where people were taking down the decorations.

I could feel every eye watching me as I joined them. From all appearances, I was a woman who had overcome her adversity. With my words and actions, I assured everyone that Devyn wasn't going to get me down. I'd be just fine without him, thank you very much. I chatted, told a few jokes and helped to take down the decorations, which were supposed to adorn the happiest day of my life. I behaved as if I had accepted the realization that I wasn't going to be Devyn's wife.

But my outside did not match what was going on inside. My heart was breaking. How could I get over the man I'd

loved for four years? True, we didn't have a perfect relationship, but I was ready to take it to the next level. I thought the love we shared was a bond that nothing or anyone could break.

But the realization that this wasn't true hurt deeply. Knowing that Devyn was—at this very moment—with someone else on the day we were supposed to be joined together as one was too much to take.

The overwhelming pain began to consume me. I knew I couldn't fake it any longer, but I had to do something. I didn't want everyone to see me collapse in agony.

Filling my voice with fake enthusiasm, I said, "You guys must be starving! Why don't you go to my mom's house and start on that banquet. Even though there wasn't a wedding, we can't take back the food, so we might as well have a party."

I only said what they wanted to do anyway. It took a few moments, but everyone finally agreed, and people started walking out to their cars.

As Tasha walked to the back of her car, she asked, "Are you coming with us?"

"You go ahead," I said as casually as I could. "I'll be there in a sec. I just want to get some more of these decorations into my car."

Tasha stared at me for a moment, shrugged, then got into her car as I crammed another load of paper wedding bells and streamers into my backseat. I waited until the last car left, then returned to the empty sanctuary.

I climbed the stairs to the balcony and took a seat in the middle of the highest pew. No longer able to keep the pain locked in, I curled into a ball and burst into tears that had been held in too long.

"Why, Lord?" I cried out. "Why doesn't Devyn love me? I really want him, Lord. I really need him. Please work this out. I don't think I can walk through this world without him. God, I will do just about anything to keep that man. Tell me what I need to do. I love him so much!"

I rocked back and forth, my shattered heart weeping loudly to the Lord. "Are You there, Lord? Can You hear me? I'm hurting so bad!"

All of the thoughts I had earlier about just wanting God's peace were gone. The only solution I could see was getting back with Devyn and making our relationship work. Being Devyn Jackson's wife was my heart's desire, and I couldn't see it any other way. I didn't want to.

"Lord, if You love me," I began, "give me the strength to do what I need to do to make this right." I looked at the big wooden cross in the pulpit. I knew God heard my words. "Thank you for being here with me, Lord. I know You will make Devyn realize what a terrible mistake he made here today."

A flash of lightning sparked outside, making me turn my attention to the window. I was surprised to see that the sky had grown dark.

I lay in the same position on the pew until the hard bench began to make my bones ache. Then I went back into the ladies' room. I needed to make myself look presentable if I was going to go to my mother's house. The mirror again revealed what a toll the day's events had taken on me. I had started out as a blushing bride and ended as a horrifying disaster.

"That's okay," I said to myself as I reapplied my mascara. "I might not look my best, but it's what's in my heart that counts. Devyn's mine, and this is all going to work out. I know he loves me. I just have to make him see it."

With my last words, the lights went out. The small, windowless bathroom was so dark I could no longer see my reflection in the mirror. I blindly stuffed my makeup back into the bag and turned to leave the room when I was startled by a voice.

"Girl, you don't know me." It was a female who spoke. "I wasn't an invited guest. I just came here 'cause I thought there might be food. But I saw what happened and I gotta tell you somethin'."

I squinted, trying to see through the darkness. I knew this woman was standing close because I could smell her breath. It reminded me of day-old fish.

"Look," the voice continued, "don't try to get that man back. You'll just make yourself look stupid if you do."

"Stupid?" I cried into the blackness. "Excuse me! I don't even know you. Please get out of here."

"Just trying to help you out," she said calmly. "But if you don't want to listen to me, maybe you'll listen to her."

The lights came on. I blinked as I looked at the only person in the bathroom with me. Aisha.

I stared at the girl Devyn had dumped me for, the mother of his child. Though I was in church, unholy thoughts filled my mind. I was ready to knock her out. Even though she was bigger, I figured I could whip her. Though I was petite, my crazy brother had taught me how to stick up for myself. And this Aisha chick definitely deserved a beat-down.

"You better be glad you're pregnant," I said, my fingers curling into tight fists.

"Glad? What do you mean by that?"

"If you weren't pregnant—"

She cocked her head and placed her hand on her hip. "Yeah, what would you do? Like you frighten me?"

"I should. Don't be fooled by what you see." I paused and looked her up and down. "Besides, maybe you're not pregnant at all!"

Her heavily painted eyes grew wide. "That's none of your business, Miss Left-at-the-Altar. Get over it."

She was begging for a beat-down, but I just said, "Well, if getting pregnant is what it takes to have a man marry you, I'd rather be alone. I don't have to trap nobody. And I know one thing. You'd better hold on because I know how Devyn feels about me. The final chapter of this book ain't been written yet."

I tried to walk around her to get out of the bathroom, but the stupid girl stepped right in front of me. When she put her hand on my arm, I snatched it with my left hand and raised my right fist to her face. "Don't try it, girl. If you touch me again, pregnant or not, I'll be all over you. And if you ever touch my man again—"

"He don't want you, remember?" Aisha said, yanking her hand out of my grasp. "He left you on your big day. Apparently you haven't been takin' care of your man, 'cause if you did, he wouldn't have been layin' up with me."

My fist dropped as if it were suddenly weighted down with lead. Aisha had a point. But there was no way she'd hear that from me.

"He's been playin' you for months." Aisha continued to spew her venom. "He wants to be with me. Shoot, when given a choice, any man would rather have steak than chicken. Devyn always did like a nice, big, juicy sirloin. Not a tiny portion half baked—"

I cut her off. "You're talking crazy."

"Oh, am I? You're the one whose trippin' 'cause Devyn don't want you no more."

"But he does want me," I screamed. "The only reason he chose you is because you told him you're carrying his child." The words caught in my throat, nearly choking me.

"That don't mean nothin'. A lot of Dev's friends got babies by girls they ain't married to. He could have married you and left me alone. But he didn't. So don't blame me 'cause he dumped you. You need to check yourself and see why he's all up on me instead of you."

"Whatever," I said, pushing past her and shoving the bathroom door open. I let it slam in her face as if that would make her vanish from my life. I knew what she was saying was foolish. "I can't let it get to me," I said, keeping myself pumped up.

I had to find my man.

I rushed to my car, this time knowing where I was headed. If Devyn wasn't with Aisha, then he was probably at home. I drove to the apartment that Devyn and Chase had shared for years.

Though Devyn held a job in Tampa, which he'd had for over a year, he still kept his place with Chase. When he came to Miami on the weekends, he had somewhere to stay. I told him he was wasting money, but he said the place wasn't that much. And he didn't want to leave his boy hanging.

Devyn and I were supposed to be moving to Tampa, where he'd landed a $40,000-a-year job. Chase was planning on leaving too, although he wasn't sure where he was going. Chase had been out of college for two years. Though he was a red-shirt freshman, he still hadn't completed his degree. He wanted to play in the NFL. Unfortunately, no pro team had picked him up. However, he was determined to keep trying. He'd applied to every training camp he could find to walk on as a free agent. Whatever that meant.

When I pulled into their apartment complex, I didn't waste a moment. I ran to their door and knocked, confident that Devyn would want to hear what I had to say. I knew my love could change his heart.

Devyn opened the door and glared at me. "What are you doing here?"

"I got some things I know you wanna hear."

"Oh, so now you want to talk? Forget it. You had your chance!" He tried to slam the door in my face, but I caught it before it closed, and stepped inside.

"Don't push me away, Devyn," I begged.

"Get out of my face," he slurred. He'd been drinking again.

"Devyn, I know you still love me. Look me in my eyes and tell me you don't want me anymore." He stared at me for a moment, then turned away. "See?" I exclaimed as if I'd just won a prize. "You can't do it. As long as you love me, Devyn, we can make this right. I forgive you for being with that girl. I love you so much that I'll love your baby, even if it isn't mine. We can make it through this."

Devyn turned around. But instead of the look of love and gratitude I'd anticipated, his eyes held disgust and contempt. "The last thing I want," he said, "is a begging woman. Do I have to come out and say it? I don't love you, Zoe. Did you hear me, girl? You ain't the one I want. You don't mean nothin' to me. I found somebody else I wanna be with, and it ain't you!"

I didn't know if he was saying those things to hurt me more, or if that was how he truly felt. But his words didn't seem right. We had too much history together. Surely he cared more than what he was showing me here.

Without thought, I pulled him into my arms, locked my hands around his ears and kissed him hard. I needed him to feel the passion that was inside me. He had to feel it, if not through my words, then through my actions.

"Dang it, girl, get off me!" Devyn yanked my arms away, then gave me a backhand slap that threw me across the room. "Man, I wish you would just go away. You are totally getting on my nerves. I can't stand this constant clinging! Don't you know that's why I was dating other girls all the time we were together?"

I stood frozen, too stunned to move. "I don't believe you, Devyn. I know you love me, and I know that I can fix this." I tried to hold back my tears. "Anyway, if I can't have you, I don't even want to live."

"So what're you gonna do? Kill yourself?" His eyes held mine. "Well, that's fine by me. Just get out of my life!"

Maybe he didn't believe me, but in that moment, I knew I didn't want to go on without him. He was everything to me, and the thought of staying in this life without him by my side was unbearable.

Wordlessly, I turned and headed for Devyn's bedroom. I opened the closet door. I knew he kept a gun stashed in a shoe box on the top shelf. I often told Devyn that I didn't like having the gun in the house. And though I often got on his case about it, he never budged. He said he wanted to make sure he could protect us in an emergency.

My hands searched the top shelf, but the shoe box was gone.

"Is this what you're looking for?" Devyn asked. I turned toward him. He was in the doorway, pulling the pistol from his duffel bag. "Here. Use it if you want." He held it out to me. "Go ahead and kill yourself. My life will go on."

I stared at the gun. In an instant, I imagined placing the barrel to my head and pulling the trigger. I could end my hopeless life.

I slowly walked toward him, keeping my eyes on the gun as if I were mesmerized. While I stared at the gun, I could feel Devyn's eyes on me, daring me to do this.

A car horn tooted outside and I stopped. My gaze moved from the gun to Devyn. With a smirk on his face, he tossed the gun onto his bed. He zipped his duffel bag and pulled the strap over his shoulder. "I'm outta here," he said. "Do whatever you want." He dashed out the door.

As I listened to his footsteps fade down the hallway, tears of despair fell from my eyes. The pain was so unbearable; my heart was being torn into tiny pieces.

I dropped to my knees beside the bed. There, right at eye level, sat the gun. I picked it up and stared at it, fondling the cold metal in my hands. My tears fell onto the trigger, and with a final sob, I placed the gun against my left temple.

I pulled the hammer back and whispered, "Lord, this may be wrong, but my life just ain't right." I paused, trying to get the words out through my tears. "I don't want to go on. I can't see my way. It's too dark."

Chapter 3

I closed my eyes. Still holding the gun to my head, I wondered what to do next. I had pulled back the hammer, but I didn't really know how to shoot it. Surely it had to be simple. Just pull the trigger, right?

I pressed my eyelids tighter; my finger trembled against the trigger. A second later, the gun was yanked from my hands. Without opening my eyes, I collapsed onto the floor and wept.

I heard the footsteps leave the room. Still, I remained withering in pain, even when I heard the footsteps return. My rescuer knelt beside me, pulled me into his arms and enveloped me in a strong embrace.

It wasn't until I heard his soft words filtering into my ear that I knew who my angel was.

"It might seem dim right now, but I'm gonna help you through this. Regardless of how you feel, you're too precious to leave this world."

"Thank you, Chase." I sobbed. "Thank you for saving my life." My body shivered. Never before had I felt so fragile, so emotionally shattered.

"It's okay," Chase said as he held me tight. "Go ahead and cry. Let Jesus hear your cry. Let Him make it better."

"What can Jesus do for me?" I gasped, feeling as if none of my prayers had been answered.

"God can fix anything. No wound is too deep for Him to mend. No scar too ugly that He can't make it beautiful. Trust me." He lifted my face with the tips of his fingers and made me look at him. "God loves you. I know you don't see anything good in yourself right now, Zoe, but in God's eyes, you're a perfect jewel. Trust Him with your life."

Chase's warm words released a further flow of tears. But even as the waves of sorrow washed over me, I realized that God had sent this angel my way to get me through this night.

It hurt that I wasn't rescued by the man I thought would be my mate for life. That guy told me he couldn't care less what I did. But in my despair, God still sent someone, and He let me see that He was still in control.

I started wiping away the tears. "You're right. I know God does care about me. He sent you. Thank you, Chase."

"You don't have to thank me." Chase planted a gentle kiss on my forehead. "I wanted to be here."

I woke up the next morning with my head nestled on Chase's chest. We were lying on the couch. He had stayed up, baby-sitting me all night long. I was glad Chase was there because I didn't know if I could have faced the day alone.

I stretched, lifting my arms in the air.

"Good morning, beautiful," Chase said as he smiled down at me. He still held me as if he didn't plan to let me go.

"I'm sure I don't look beautiful right now," I said, trying to untangle my hair with my fingers.

"You're always beautiful in my eyes. Why should today be any different?"

His words didn't surprise me. He was always saying things to make me feel better—always cleaning up after Devyn.

Chase got off the couch and headed for the kitchen. "This is going to be a great day. I can feel it."

I watched as Chase filled the coffeepot with water and then set it on the coffee stand. He moved with such excitement and expectancy; I didn't understand. I wondered how he could feel so confident. After everything I went through the day before, there was no way this day could possibly be great.

"Come on," Chase encouraged. "I'm making you breakfast."

I wasn't hungry, but Chase was so happy and had done so much to help me, I wanted to keep him smiling. So I sat at the table, sipping my coffee and nibbling on my wheat toast.

I tried to smile and chat, but my thoughts kept returning to yesterday—the day that was supposed to be the best in my life, yet had turned into the worst.

"Okay," Chase said when he cleaned off the table. "We're going out."

I didn't have enough energy to protest. So, after he brought my suitcases inside, I showered and changed.

"Where are we going?" I asked when I joined Chase in the living room.

He took my hand and pulled me from the couch. "Just come with me."

We walked to Virginia Key Beach and Chase pointed out where he liked to work out. Then we strolled to the sand and sat down. For minutes, we watched the waves crash along the shore.

"I might be playing in the NFL this season," Chase announced suddenly.

My eyes moved from the unsettling waves to Chase. When I saw his smile, my lips turned up into one of my own. "What! For real!" I exclaimed. I took his hand and squeezed it.

"Yeah, after a year of all this training and calling all those teams, the Seattle Storm gave me a positive response. They may be offering me a free-agent contract."

I paused for just a moment. "Devyn told me you couldn't make a team, that you're not fast enough." Just mentioning my man's name almost caused my tears to flow once again.

"Oh, yeah?" Chase countered. "Since when does that guy know anything? Watch this!"

Suddenly he stood and sprinted up the beach while I sat, embraced by the soothing sand. I watched the muscles ripple down his dark back. His well-toned thighs carried him gracefully, yet speedily. Even his butt caught my attention, and my, oh my, was it fine! Actually for the first time, I realized Chase was a cutie. His sweet, dark chocolate skin tempted me to want to lick him all over.

Quickly, shaking my head, I dismissed the naughty thoughts from my mind. I knew that Chase liked me, and one move from me could put us in a relationship. But I couldn't lead Chase on. Even though Devyn cared nothing for me, I was still in love with him. I was too wounded to consider another love. Besides, Devyn and Chase had been tight for years.

Still, seeing Chase the way I did gave me hope that another man besides Devyn could be pleasing in my sight. I hadn't thought that would ever be the case.

As Chase sprinted back toward me, I saw determination written all over his face. I had a feeling that the Seattle Storm had no idea how valuable Chase would be to their team.

When he reached me, he kicked sand onto my legs.

"Stop," I said, not really wanting him to. "I hope they call. You deserve a shot."

"Thanks. That means a lot." He grabbed my hand and pulled me up. "Look at you! You're all sandy," he joked. "You gotta get cleaned up now." He dragged me into the cool ocean water.

We were acting like a couple of high-school kids on a first date. But this was not a date, I reminded myself.

We spent the rest of the day acting like tourists, enjoying lunch at one of the cafés on the beach and then browsing through the boutiques. We couldn't buy anything because neither one of us had a dime to spare. As the sun set, we walked along the ocean's line until the day bowed to night.

Then we went to the Rusty Pelican for dinner. We sat at a candlelit table as a jazz ensemble softly played in the corner. The atmosphere was completely romantic. But the flickering candlelight and the background music only reminded me that I was supposed to be on my honey-moon.

"What's wrong?" Chase asked as he reached across the table and placed his hand over mine.

I thought back to the hours we'd spent together and the million little things Chase had done to make me laugh and feel special throughout the entire day. Now, I appreciated him trying to console me, but I was still a mess. There wasn't anything special about me, and I knew it; this had to be why Devyn had rejected me.

I stared at him for a moment before I stood from the table and ran, almost bumping into the waiter who was just bringing our dinners. I wasn't in great shape like Chase, but I still made it back to his apartment first, proba-bly because he had to give some explanation to the waiter.

But it wasn't until I arrived that I realized I didn't have the key. I pounded on the door, not because I expected to be answered, but because I was filled with frustration, anger and sadness.

"Why, Lord?" I shouted. "Why is all this happening to me?"

I don't know how long I stood there, sobbing against the door, before Chase came behind me and pressed his face against my neck. That sweet gesture let me know that he felt my pain. He shared it, cared about it and didn't want me to have to experience it. I so appreciated his compas-sion, but I couldn't let go of my grief.

Minutes later, Chase opened the door and led me inside. We sat on the couch, and he held me silently until my tears stopped.

"Are you okay?" he whispered when he saw my tear-free face.

I nodded, though I really didn't think I'd be okay ever again.

"I promise, Zoe, it's going to be all right. You'll look back on this one day and know that it all happened for a purpose."

I nodded again, not because I agreed with him, but because there was no need to argue.

"You haven't talked to your mother today, have you?" Chase asked.

I shook my head.

"I'm sure she's worried by now." He stood, lifted the cordless phone from the table and handed it to me.

I knew Chase was right. I needed to let the people who cared about me know that I was okay. But I didn't want anyone to come looking for me. Not just yet.

I took the phone from Chase. "I'll call my brother."

Chase nodded and sat on the couch as I dialed the number.

"Alonzo, it's me," I said when he answered the phone on the first ring.

"Zoe, girl, 'bout time. We've been worried 'bout you."

"I know. I'm sorry. But I'm fine."

"Where you at?"

I was grateful that he didn't have caller ID. "I'm safe." I glanced at Chase sideways. "And I'm with someone who cares about me and can take care of me."

Chase smiled.

"Like I don't? I care about you too, Zoe," Alonzo said with a sigh.

"I know. But I just need a few days. Do me a favor and let Mom and everyone know that I'm straight."

My brother was hesitant. I knew he didn't agree. Finally, after a long pause, he agreed to pass on the message. Pressing the off button, Chase pulled me into his arms. I slept like a baby as he held me.

The following days flew by in a blur. My life felt strange, as if I were going through withdrawal from a drug. I even got the chills from time to time. Chase nurtured me as if I were an addict—making sure that I ate and slept. He took care of my every need. But he couldn't help me purge Devyn from my system. I had to get the jerk out of my heart, but it was so difficult to shake the feeling of love I'd held for him for such a long time.

Three days after I talked to my brother, Chase gave me some news that sent me spinning.

"I got accepted into the Seattle Storm's training camp," he announced as he placed a paper plate bearing a ham sandwich in front of me. "I told the landlord I'd be out of the apartment by the end of the month."

I stared at him, my mouth open wide. Finally, words came out. "What am I going to do?" All kinds of thoughts went through my mind. I still didn't have a job, or even the prospect of one. I didn't have anyplace to live. I'd given up everything to be Devyn's wife. But what frightened me the most was trying to do this recovery without Chase. "I've leaned on you so much this last week. Not havin' you here is kinda scary."

Chase sat down across from me. "I wish I didn't have to go so soon," he said, his voice husky. "I don't want to leave if you're not capable of handling things. I wouldn't want you to get so depressed that you'd contemplate . . . what you thought about on Saturday."

I shook my head. "Don't be silly. I wouldn't do that again," I assured him. But his glance told me that he wasn't sure. Though I didn't want him to go, I knew I had to let him know that I'd be okay. "You've already done more for me than I could ever ask, Chase. Besides, you have to go. I want you to be successful and prove Devyn wrong." We shared a refreshing laugh that lightened the oppressive mood. But though I tried to reassure him, I couldn't make myself feel better. "Chase, I'm not sure I can find my way without you."

"Zoe, the battle's not yours," he said. "You gotta let go of this idea that you need a guy to take care of you. The only one you really need to lead you is God."

Deep down, I knew Chase was right. I hadn't done much praying since my wedding day disaster. I felt like God had abandoned me, so why should I talk to Him? I had believed His promise that He would give me the desires of my heart. Devyn was my greatest desire, and losing him made me extremely bitter.

"I know you mean well and all, Chase," I said, trying not to sound rude. "But I really don't want to hear any preachin' right now, okay?"

"Why? Because God didn't do what you wanted Him to do?"

I looked at Chase and wondered, how could this man see so keenly into my mind and voice my thoughts so clearly?

"Zoe, God is always in control. He does things for our good, even though sometimes we can't see it. Isn't it better for Him to give you what you need, instead of what you think you want?"

"All I want is to have Devyn in my life! How can wanting to be on my honeymoon be so wrong? Don't I need to know where my life is going? Doesn't God need to do at least that for me?"

"Listen," Chase said calmly. "I love God, not because of what He does for me, but because of who He is. He's my Savior, my Redeemer and my Lord."

"I'm glad that works for you." Trying not to hear all that, I took a bite of my sandwich.

"I guess what I'm trying to say, Zoe, is that the things I ask God for are the things that please Him. I want His will to be done in my life more than I want my desires to be met. If I desire His will, then everything I want will be done."

I had no interest in what Chase was yakking about. Truth be told, I didn't want to listen. But I wasn't going to tell him to be quiet, and he kept talking. It was his sincerity that forced me to tune in.

"A lot of folks go around saying, '*I want God to bless my relationship. I want this man or that woman.*' Then they go fornicating all through the relationship. They ignore the fact that God asks us to be clean. How in the world can they expect Him to bless their relationship when they don't do what He says?"

It was hard to swallow the bit of sandwich that was in my mouth. I wondered how much Chase knew about the level of intimacy there'd been in my relationship with Devyn. I was sure Dev had bragged about his conquest. Suddenly I felt ashamed of the things he had undoubtedly told his roommate. I lowered my eyes, unable to look at Chase.

"Zoe, Devyn doesn't even know God. But you do. You may not be where you need to be in your walk because you're hurt and angry right now. But deep down, I know you love the Lord. And God doesn't want you to be with somebody who doesn't love Him. He can't bless a relationship that's not built on His principles."

I didn't know what to say, so I just kept eating. I noticed Chase hadn't touched his food.

Chase kept talking, and after a few minutes, I could tell that he seemed to be getting frustrated, maybe even angry. He seemed upset that I could not see what he was saying. That I didn't really get it. That I was holding on to my troubles. I could tell that Chase was disappointed and that bothered me. Although I owed him nothing, I didn't want to let him down.

Finally, Chase pushed back his chair from the table, his ham sandwich still untouched. "I gotta get ready to go to the airport," he muttered.

My gaze shot up to his face. "Already?" I shrieked, fear obvious in my voice. "You can't be leaving today?" I glanced into the living room. There were no bags, no signs of his preparing to go anywhere. But that only meant that he had probably packed in his bedroom. I'd been sleeping in Devyn's bed.

"My flight leaves tonight," he explained. "I have my first workout tomorrow morning."

I tried to swallow my fear, but it stuck in my throat. "Well, I guess I'd better get my things together and get out of here too." I couldn't begin to answer the questions that ran through my mind: *Where am I going to go? What am I supposed to do?*

"There's no need for you to rush. The rent is paid up till the end of the month. You might as well stay here until then."

I breathed, but I wasn't totally relieved. "How will I get in touch with you?"

"Until I know how things are going to work in training camp, I won't have a number I can give you. I'll call whenever I can, but I've got to really focus on trying to make this team."

"I understand." I didn't like it, but I understood. I wasn't his responsibility.

Chase went to his bedroom and I stared at his untouched sandwich. I took our dishes to the kitchen sink and wrapped his lunch in cellophane. I was grateful for the activity. I needed something to do as I processed this information. By the time I finished cleaning the kitchen, Chase returned with three suitcases. He placed them by the door.

"Chase," I said, "I don't want you to be mad at me. I really appreciate everything you've done for me." I wrapped my arms around him and held him tight.

He opened his mouth to speak, but before he could release his words, the front door burst open. Startled, I released my hold on Chase, but not soon enough.

"What's up with this?" Devyn ranted, throwing his hands in the air. "My boy gettin' it on with my ex? Dang! Well, you can have her, man. I don't care. I just came to pick up a few things." Devyn stormed through the house, grabbing his towels and other bathroom gear, getting the rest of his funky clothes, which had been on the floor of his closet for nearly a week, and some kitchen appliances that I'd bought for him. He stuffed all that into a big black duffel bag, continuing his verbal rampage as he moved from room to room. "And you wonder why I don't want you no more, Zoe? Look at you, girl. The minute I'm gone, you go and get with my best man. I can just imagine how wrong you'd have done me if we got married." Devyn tossed a coffee mug into the bag so hard something shattered inside. He didn't even pause. "And Chase, my brotha'. I figured you were a trip. I knew you weren't no good. You always wanted my woman. Well, I'm done with her, man. I done throwed out this piece of trash. If you want it, it's yours!"

In that moment, it occurred to me that I had been moping over a guy who not only didn't care about me but was so arrogant he made me sick. For the first time, I really looked at Devyn. And what I saw made my stomach turn.

I was finally seeing another side of this man, or maybe a side that had always been there, but I was too blind to see before. I knew now that Chase was right. I should have been down on my knees, thanking God for not allowing us to be life partners. I needed to thank God for showing me what this man was really like.

Now I had hope—hope of getting over Devyn and moving on with my life. This scene wasn't what I'd call showers of blessings, but I was thankful for the safe harbor Chase offered me, the lull.

Chapter 4

Red-hot anger tensed Chase's body as he watched Devyn stomp and shout through the apartment. I wasn't sure which of Devyn's words ticked Chase off, but before I could do anything, he lunged toward Devyn, ready to punch him out. I quickly jumped, standing between the two friends. My action made Chase stop. He placed his trembling arms around me.

I turned around and looked at Devyn. He was staring at Chase and me—or should I say, he was staring at our embrace. His eyes were sad, appearing full of hurt that Chase and I stood that way, holding each other. But he put on a tough face, seeming to pretend it didn't matter. Without a word, he disappeared into his bedroom.

Chase still held me, his arms tight around my waist, and I understood Devyn's sadness. I wasn't sure what the hug meant myself. As Chase held me, I couldn't deny my feelings for him—it was as if a surge of passion filled me.

But I had to keep my feelings inside, at least for the moment.

Chase gazed into my eyes, his arms still in place. "The airport shuttle will be here any minute, and if I don't catch it, I'll miss my plane," he said softly.

I trembled.

"But I can reschedule my flight for the morning if you don't want to be here alone with him."

I didn't want Chase to leave at all. When he walked out that door, whether it happened tonight or in the morning, he would be going to a world far away from me.

Though I wasn't in love with Chase, I did love him. And over the past days, I'd grown to love him more than I ever thought could happen. He was my anchor holding me together, helping me find peace in turbulent seas. I still couldn't get used to the thought of not having him around.

But again, I wanted him to know that it was okay to leave. Chase had done his job. It was time for me to stand up and do mine. I didn't know how I was going to survive without him, but deep down I knew I could.

Just as I had that thought, we heard a van's horn and I knew it was the shuttle.

"Go," I said. Then I kissed him on the cheek. "Thanks for caring. Don't worry about me. I'm gonna be fine."

He nodded, though I could tell that he didn't want to leave. He wasn't sure. He said, "I'll call you the first chance I get."

"I'd like that," I said softly. "Now, go on." I turned him around and nudged him toward the door. "Make me proud."

He grabbed the doorknob and one suitcase, then paused. "You take care of yourself, okay? Here." He handed me his Bible from his bag. "Open God's Word. It will protect you."

I chuckled slightly. "And where should I start, Chase? I haven't read the Bible in a long time."

"Just open it. Or go to a passage you know. I bet God will speak to your soul." With his free hand, he touched my cheek. "Will you do that for me, Zoe?"

"I'll do it tonight," I promised. "Now, go catch your plane."

I watched as he took two bags to the shuttle, then came back for the third one. But after he picked up the suitcase, he paused. He looked at me, then lowered his gaze to the ground. I could tell he wanted to say more, but no words could escape from his juicy lips.

Feeling the awkwardness, I said, "You just be sure and come back, okay?"

"Count on it." With a final glance of warmth toward me, he stepped outside.

The minute the door closed, I raced to the window and watched Chase climb into the royal blue bus with yellow lettering. I stayed until the shuttle pulled away.

In my heart, I wished him the best of luck. Yet, at the same time, I wished the shuttle would stop suddenly and make a U-turn, bringing Chase back to me.

"He gone, babe." Devyn interrupted my thoughts. "Starin' out the window ain't gonna bring him back."

Without turning away from the window, I said, "Devyn, get out."

"Yeah, right. My name's on the lease, baby, not yours."

I whipped around to face him. "But you moved out, remember? And I'm staying here now. Chase told me I could. So you just get out and go to your pregnant fiancée. Spare us both the agony of having to deal with one another."

He sauntered up to me, his face filled with a sly grin. He slipped his hands around my waist. "C'mon, baby. What do you say we get it on one more time? You know, for old time's sake."

I lifted my hand to slap him, but he grabbed my wrist and stopped me.

"Watch yourself now," he warned, though he still smiled as if he weren't in the least bit threatened by my gesture.

"You make me sick."

"Oh, really?" he said, releasing my arm but not my waist. "Just 'cause I wouldn't stop you from shooting your dumb self?"

All my feelings of insecurity that I had worked so hard to release over the past few days rushed back, filling my soul. I couldn't let Devyn make me feel vulnerable again. I needed strength.

Lord, I prayed inside through my anger, *get this jerk out of my face. Please.*

Suddenly Devyn turned around, picked up his duffel bag and walked out the door. Again I found myself at the window, watching as Devyn hopped into his car and peeled out of the parking lot.

I stayed at the window for minutes before finally turning and looking around the room. For the first time in almost a week, I was alone. I wondered what I should do first.

I figured I could call my mother, even though I'd just spoken to my brother a few days ago. I knew my mother was concerned, but not really worried. Even though we hadn't spoken in days, this wasn't unusual. Mom and I rarely talked. I had long ago accepted the fact that she was my mother, not my friend.

Still, I didn't want her to see how torn up I was. She had tried to raise me to be a strong woman, and over the past several days, I'd been anything but strong. But I didn't like the feeling of being alone, and since I was unable to come up with anything else to do, I picked up the phone.

"Hey, Ma," I said when she answered.

"Baby! Zoe, girl, where have you been? I've been worried sick."

"I know, Ma. I'm sorry."

"I called everybody I could think of, but no one knew what happened to you."

"Didn't Alonzo call you?"

"Yes, but he didn't really tell me anything except that you had called and said you were fine. But where are you, baby?"

"Not too far away. I'm still in Miami. I needed some time to myself."

"I understand that, but, child, I've been goin' plumb crazy wonderin' what's going on."

"You don't have to worry, Mom. I'm all right. I'm getting a new perspective on the whole situation."

"Baby, I hate not knowing where you are or what you're doing. Why don't you just come home?"

I paused for a moment, thinking about what it would be like to be living with my mother again—especially after all I'd been through. "Mom, I'm not ready to do that. I know you love me and you're trying to help, but I really need the time by myself to clear my head." When I heard my mother sigh, I continued. "But there is something you can do for me, Mom."

"Okay, baby." She perked up, eager to help me through in any way she could.

"Pray for me, okay? Keep me lifted up before the Lord. That's what I really need."

"That sounds good and fine, baby," she said, sounding disappointed. "But God's got your mama here to do more than that. I need to take care of you. Now, you need to come on home."

I sighed. My mother could be so exasperating some-times! This was one of the reasons I hardly ever talked to her. "Look, Ma," I started, needing to explain my point. "I have to quit depending on other people and let God take care of me," I said, thinking of what Chase had said to me earlier. "I need to give Him a chance to be Lord of my life." As I said the words, I realized how true they were. I knew I had been on quite a roller-coaster ride—first wanting to depend on God, then not wanting to talk to Him at all. But now I knew where I wanted to be—I wanted to rely solely on Christ. I longed for that to be my reality, to be what I truly lived.

"You ain't talkin' to that dog Devyn, are ya?" my mother whined. "You know you gotta let that go."

I rolled my eyes. *Where did that come from?* I wondered. Here I was talking about Christ and making Him the center of my life, and my mother was talking about Devyn. Besides, even if Devyn wasn't the best man I could end up with, he'd still given me much more than Mom's string of men had ever given her. "Mom, I'm really not in the mood for a lecture. I know you care, but I just don't want to hear it. I don't mean any disrespect, but I can't handle this right now." I paused, but only for a moment. Then I said quickly, "I love you, Mom, but I gotta go."

Hanging up the phone while my mother was still yakking was a difficult thing to do, but I didn't have any other choice.

I tossed the phone onto the table and sat on the living-room sofa. The apartment felt more than empty without Chase. But I knew I had to learn to adjust to the solitude. I expected to be alone quite a bit from now on.

I lay back, closed my eyes and thought about the things I'd told my mother—about depending solely on Christ. I'd always relied on other people for everything, from taking care of me to making me happy, but sinful human beings were far from perfect. I never fully realized how easily they could let me down.

But giving everything to Christ, letting Him be in control, was a new concept to me. I really wanted to do that, but I needed a road map.

I opened my eyes and stared at the Bible sitting on the coffee table. I knew I should read it, like I'd promised Chase. But I really didn't know where to start, so I closed my eyes again.

I couldn't get the thoughts of God from my mind. I really wanted to find direction for my life. I'd been running in a million different ways but not really going anywhere.

Finally, I sat up and lifted the heavy book. I opened it to the table of contents. I turned to Psalms and found the twenty-third chapter, one that was familiar to me.

"'The Lord is my shepherd. I shall not want,'" I read out loud, my voice sounding strange in the quiet room. I stopped right there and read that passage over and over again.

Just that verse was an answer to a prayer for me; I thought of all the things I'd been wanting. Devyn. The perfect wedding. A job. A mother who understood me. Chase's presence in my life. A home of my own. But the two short sentences on the page before me assured me that if Christ was truly my shepherd, I didn't have to want for anything. He would supply all of my needs. I realized then that God would not give me everything I wanted because sometimes what I wanted wasn't what was best for me. Like Devyn—God knew all along that Devyn wasn't the man I needed, even though I couldn't see that for myself because I was so blinded by what I thought was love.

I read the Scripture again, claiming the verse for myself. "'The Lord is my shepherd. I shall not want.'"

That was all I needed.

I placed the open Bible back on the coffee table, then slipped off the couch and got to my knees. "Father," I said, "I've been going back and forth over what to do with my life. I still don't have the answers, but I know You do. You know exactly where I'm going and where You want to take me. I now release custody of my life to You. Please do whatever You know is best for me. Thank you for assuring me that I can trust You and not worry. You're not like me, changing from one day to the next. One minute to the next, really. But You are a constant God who loves and cares for me, no matter what. I need Your love right now."

Tears began to build up behind my closed eyelids as I realized how wretched I was. I felt so unworthy. Why should God love me? "Lord, I feel so empty. I'm so weary and weak. I need You." As a salty teardrop slid down my cheek, I sensed the Lord wrapping me in His arms, whispering words of love and assurance in my ear. I felt His presence more tangibly than anything I'd ever experienced in my life. "Thank you, Lord," I said, repeating the phrase over and over.

I climbed back onto the couch and lay down. I closed my eyes. I wanted to rest—for just a few minutes—before I decided what to do with the rest of the evening. But once I closed my eyes, I fell into a deep slumber. And, for the first time in a week, I enjoyed a peaceful night's sleep.

When I awakened, the sun was already shining brightly through the window and I smiled, stretching and feeling totally rested. I went into the kitchen and opened the refrigerator. There was plenty of grub. I guess Chase was looking out for me when he filled up the fridge. Even though I eyed the eggs, bacon and sausages, I didn't feel like spending time over the stove. So I loaded a plate with cookless munchies: some sweet cut cantaloupe, two glazed chocolate doughnuts and a piece of bologna. Then I curled up on the couch with the remote and flipped through the channels, cruising from one talk show to the next. I watched all the soap operas I could find.

That became my routine for the next several days. I lounged around the apartment, enjoying the luxury of having nothing to do and no one to answer to. Although I was enjoying the mindless days, I kept thinking about Chase and wishing that he would call. I knew he was busy getting settled not only with the team but with Seattle in general. Yet I just couldn't wait to hear his voice again.

Almost a week after Chase left, the phone rang in the middle of one of my talk shows and I jumped, startled at first. The telephone hadn't rung since he'd been gone. But I knew it was Chase. It had to be. No one else knew I was here.

"Hey, guy!" I said, my voice revealing my enthusiasm.

"Oh, so you expectin' my man to call you, huh?" I didn't catch the voice at first, but when I realized it was Aisha, I was so surprised that I remained silent. "Well, let me 'splain somethin' to ya, Little Miss Thang. That is not the way it's gonna be. What part of 'I don't wanna marry you no more 'cause I got somebody else' do you not understand?"

"I don't know what you're talking about," I said. "But I don't need you callin' me with this drama." I slammed the phone down.

She had some nerve! Thinking I still wanted Devyn after all his junk. Before I could calm myself down, the phone rang again. I grabbed the receiver. I didn't even have the chance to say hello before Aisha started screaming into the phone. "How dare you hang up on me. I got somethin' to say to you."

"Well, I got nothin' to say to you, girl," I yelled back, holding the phone so tight my knuckles hurt. "And I'll hang up on you anytime I like!" I slammed the phone so hard this time that I wondered if I'd broken the receiver. It didn't matter—I didn't care.

Almost immediately, the phone rang again. I thought about jerking the cord from the wall and throwing it across the room, but instead I took a deep breath, trying to regain my composure. Aisha obviously wasn't getting the hint.

I picked up the phone on the third ring and hollered: "Why aren't you getting this, you moron? I don't want to talk to you!"

Just before I slammed the receiver back onto its base with a thud, I heard Chase's sexy voice floating through the line. "Man," he said, "I thought you'd be missing me by now."

I pulled the phone back to my ear.

He said, "Well, since you don't wanna talk to me, I guess I'll just hang up."

"Chase," I cried. "How are you? How's camp? What's going on? Do you like Seattle? How does the team look?"

He laughed. "Hey, let me answer one question before you throw out seventeen more. And anyway, who did you think I was? Calling me a moron!"

"Never mind about that." I had forgotten all about Aisha. Chase had erased that situation, just with the sound of his voice. I wanted to climb through the phone line and hug him. "I've been waiting to hear from you. How have you been?"

"It's been something," he declared, but his tone was full of cheer.

I sat on the couch and listened intently as he told me about his routine: waking up at five in the morning for meetings, then going out on the field for practice. Then it was back to meetings. After the team dinner, the day ended with more meetings. "The night meetings usually last till around ten," Chase said. "Sometimes twelve, depending on what the coach thought about the workout."

It sounded grueling to me. But I could tell Chase was loving it. "So, the Seattle Storm, huh? You know, I've always been more into college football than the NFL, but if I recall, that team's not too pitiful," I teased.

He chuckled. "They used to be great. Until about three years ago, when they lost their best receiver to free agency. Still, working out for this team is a great opportunity. They have twelve wide receivers here in camp, and they're probably only gonna keep five or six. So neither the politics nor the statistics are on my side. But I'm grateful to even be here."

"You're a great wide receiver, Chase. Probably better than any guy out there."

"Thank you, Zoe. You know I believe that," he said with confidence. "But the pro league is different from college. They got the best of the best here. I know I'm good, but everybody here is great. And some of these guys got big signing bonuses and contracts already. So I don't know how this is gonna work out. But you know what? The Lord knows, and that's good enough for me." Without waiting for my reaction to his comment, he said, "But that's enough talk about football. How are you doing?"

"I'm good," I said. Part of me wanted to tell him that I'd been thinking about him constantly, but I didn't want to appear too aggressive. Besides, I still didn't fully understand where all these feelings for Chase were coming from, and I didn't know what would happen if I revealed my feelings to him. We'd been good friends for a long time, and I didn't know if taking our relationship to another level was what he wanted. If we did get more intimate, could we still remain friends?

"So, are you going to tell me why you answered the phone the way you did?" he asked again.

"Oh, don't worry about that." I really didn't want to talk about Aisha. I only had a few precious minutes with Chase and I wasn't going to waste them talking about Devyn's whore. "So, what do you do in your free time? Check out the Seattle females?"

"Free time?" He chuckled. "Every minute I got, I'm in my play book trying to study. It's all I can do to find time to get on my knees and pray every day."

I noticed he didn't say he'd been thinking of me. But I understood how stressed out he was. The only thing he could think about was football. "Look, I know you don't have much time to spare, so I'll let you go. But I'm really glad you called."

"I just wanted to let you know I made it here okay. I'll be in touch. Take care of yourself, okay?"

"I will," I promised.

I hung up the phone and looked around the living room. Empty soda cans, napkins, wrappers and used paper plates were scattered throughout and I realized that I'd been wasting all my time eating and watching TV. That had to change.

I spent the rest of the week cleaning up the apartment. When I woke up on Sunday, it was spotless. I tossed the jeans that I'd been wearing into a laundry basket and put on a casual pantsuit. Then for the first time in over a week, I headed out the door. My first stop was going to be the grocery store to pick up some healthy snacks and a newspaper, hopefully filled with classified job ads.

But when I got to my car, I noticed that my two back tires were completely flat. "This is ridiculous," I groaned, kicking one of the tires as if my venting would make it return to its normal size. What could I have run over that would have put holes in not only one tire but two?

I walked to the front of my car. Those two tires were fine. It was strange. Then, a second later, it hit me. Aisha!

"Why can't that crazy chick leave me alone?" I fumed out loud. I stormed back into the apartment and called the police.

"I want to report a crime," I said. "And I'm pretty sure I know who did it!"

"Please hold," the operator said.

I waited for ages, listening to stupid elevator music and tapping my foot. I was getting angrier by the minute.

I don't know how long I was waiting, when I heard a knock on the door. The Muzak was still playing in my ear, so I hung up. I would take care of Aisha later.

I opened the door and stood shocked, but only for a moment. I tried to press the door closed, but Aisha held out her hand just in time.

"Get away from this door!" I hollered. "You already done cut my tires. Ain't that enough for one day?"

"You're trippin', girl! First you don't wanna speak to me on the phone and now you're tryin' to slam the door in my face. What's wrong with you?"

"What's wrong with me?" I screamed. "You're what's wrong with me, you lunatic!"

"Lunatic? Look, we need to talk."

"And why should I talk to your crazy behind, you tire slasher?"

"Hey, I didn't cut your tires," she said.

"Oh, okay. So I'm stupid now? I got dummy written across my forehead? Go tell it to somebody who believes your crazy lies."

"Well, I got some things to say to you. So you gonna let me in, or we gonna stand here hollerin' at each other, huh?"

I crossed my arms in front of me, not budging.

"Look, Zoe, I ain't done nothin' to your tires. You gotta learn not to accuse folks without proof to back you up."

"So, are you saying you did it, but there just ain't any evidence to prove it?"

"No," said Aisha, but a shiftiness in her eyes told me she was lying. "I ain't sayin' nothin'. 'Cept that you need to stop tryin' to get back with my man!"

"What are you talkin' about? It's over with me and Devyn. Clearly over. The last time I saw him, he was here only for a few minutes to pick up his junk—"

"Yeah, right," Aisha cut in. "He came over here several times last week to get the rest of his stuff. And I'm sure you remember the last time. Especially since you took off all your clothes and wouldn't let him leave. You got a lot of nerve, girl, tryin' to force yourself on my man."

Now I knew that both Devyn and Aisha were crazy. "What? You can't be serious!" I couldn't believe the stories that Devyn had been telling his girlfriend.

"Then yesterday he came home with hickeys all over his neck. Girl, I ain't stupid. I know you put them there."

"Oh, so he just let me put hickeys on his neck, huh?"

"You callin' my man a liar?"

"You figure it out. As far as I can tell, that boy's pullin' the same mess on you that he gave me for years. I never saw it till it was too late. I was a real fool. Seems pretty obvious that you're one now too."

"Don't you go callin' me no fool, girl!"

When she stepped back to swing at me, I pushed the door closed, locking it right away. Shaking with fury, I crossed to the window and stayed there until I saw Aisha finally slump into her car and drive away.

I rushed into the kitchen, found the phone book and scanned the Yellow Pages. I called until I found a tire shop that was not only open on Sunday but also credit-card friendly. It took less than an hour for the tow truck to come, taking me and my car to the shop.

"How long will this take?" I asked the mechanic.

He looked me up and down, making me shift uncomfortably. "Not too long. What? You're in a hurry?"

I shook my head. I didn't want to make the man who was going to work on my car mad, so I just returned to the waiting room. I sighed, knowing that it would take at least an hour and I would be totally bored. But then I noticed the newspaper stand. I bought a paper and immediately turned to the classified section, searching through the employment ads. But even though I studied all the listings from accountant to zoologist, I didn't find anything that I was qualified for or that looked at all interesting.

"Are you looking for a job, little lady?"

I looked up at the mechanic leering at me.

"Is my car ready?"

He nodded, and I gave him my credit card. It seemed to take forever for him to ring it up, but when he handed me my keys, I rushed out of there.

When I got back to the apartment, I changed my clothes and then plopped onto the couch, ready just to watch TV. Then I didn't really want to do that anymore, so I went into the bedroom. Since I had never unpacked, I had to go through my suitcases, pulling out the outfits that I thought would be appropriate for a job interview, if I ever found something worth applying for.

As I lifted my red dress in front of me and looked in the mirror, I realized what a mess my hair was. My hibernation and sudden cleaning spree left me looking like a wreck. I needed to take care of myself so I'd feel better about wherever God was going to take me. I spent the rest of the night washing and pressing my clothes and trying to bring more order into my life.

First thing the next morning, I called Keisha. My hairstylist was one of the few who worked on Mondays, and she told me she could squeeze me in if I came right away.

"Ooh, child," Keisha squealed as she washed my hair twenty minutes later. "I can't thank you enough for giving me all those referrals. How many bridesmaids did you have? About seven?"

"Yeah," I said, trying not to think about that awful day. I wondered why she would bring up the subject. I was sure that everyone already knew what Devyn had done to me.

Keisha picked up on my misery. "I'm so sorry you got left at the altar like that," she said, rubbing my head with a towel.

"Yeah, it wasn't cool." I squirmed in my seat. I could feel every eye in the shop turning toward me, and they were all filled with pity.

Keisha didn't seem to notice my embarrassment. "I heard that Aisha girl was in a gang once. But I never found out if the rumor was true."

Keisha led me to her stylist chair. I didn't respond to her comment at all, hoping this would give her a hint.

"Your girlfriend said you should've known," Keisha continued as she combed out my hair. "She said that boy cheated on you all through college, but you stayed with him anyway."

I felt the tears coming to my eyes.

"Girl, once a dog, always a dog. Like I always try to tell the ladies that come in here, you gotta keep your eyes open."

I prayed that she would just stop talking.

"We women can't afford to be naive these days. But your friend said that's what you were—naive."

"Who told you all this stuff?" I cried, not able to hold it inside anymore.

"Now, you hold still, dear," Keisha said, grabbing the sides of my head and positioning me. "How short do you want it?"

I couldn't believe Keisha didn't understand. "I don't care," I said. "Just make it look nice."

Keisha pulled a long pair of scissors from a drawer and

scrutinized my face, her head tilted. Then, with a decisive nod, she started chopping away.

"So?" I pressed. "Who told you all that stuff about Devyn?"

"I think she was your matron of honor. Well, maid of honor," Keisha corrected herself. "She came in here the other day just flappin' her gums about you."

I sat dumbfounded, staring at the mirror before me but not really seeing anything. How could Tasha, my best friend, have been so casual about spreading my business all over town? I knew we had issues, but this kind of betrayal really hurt.

"You know, I thought y'all were tighter than that," Keisha said as if she could read my mind. "But you know how folks are. Smile up in your face, then talk behind your back. It ain't right. But you sure ain't the only one. I lost my best friend when I took over this shop."

"You mean Chantay?" I asked. I didn't really care who Keisha was talking about, but I was glad to be talking about someone else's problems.

"Oh, yeah. You notice she don't work here no more. When the owner sold this shop to me, Chantay got mad and left. Couldn't stand to see me do good. That sounds like the same mess you're in. Your girlfriend seemed almost happy that you got embarrassed; I guess 'cause she wasn't the one gettin' married."

I just nodded, annoyed that the conversation had come back to me.

"Now, please don't tell her I said nothin', 'cause she's been in here a couple of times since the weddin', so don't mess up my money. But I'm tellin' ya on the sly, Zoe, that girl ain't your friend."

For the three hours I sat in that shop, I thought about what Keisha had said. Tasha wasn't my friend. And as I drove home with those thoughts still consuming me, my pulse raced and my breathing quickened. First Devyn, then Aisha. Now Tasha. I couldn't take much more of this pressure. It was coming from all different directions. I needed a release. I needed to get away. But where could I go? What could I do? Whom did I have to turn to? I couldn't even trust my best friend.

I rushed into the apartment and went straight to Chase's Bible. I opened it again to the Twenty-third Psalm. But instead of reading just the first line, I went a little further.

"'The Lord is my shepherd,'" I read out loud. "'I shall not want. He maketh me to lie down in green pastures.'"

Ha! That's a trip, I thought. My grass seemed brown and dead.

"'He leadeth me beside the still waters.'"

That's another thing that's not true for me. I got a whole lot of waves ragin' in my life right now. "Father," I prayed, "I need You to say, 'Peace; be still' to all these crazy situations I'm going through."

Before I could read or pray further, I heard a rattling noise in the back room. I looked up, startled. What now? An intruder?

My heart pounded as I heard footsteps coming from the back. My eyes darted around the room, searching for anything that I could use as a weapon. I grabbed my purse. With as much junk as I had in it, I could probably knock someone out cold, or at least give him a good scare. My eyes opened wide when the intruder entered the living room.

"Chase!"

He looked at me blankly.

"What are you doing here?"

"I live here, remember?"

"What happened to training camp?"

He slumped over to the couch. "I got released. Coach let me go."

I sat beside him and noticed how bad he looked. His red eyes were weary and it looked like he hadn't shaved in a couple of days. I could imagine how he felt. To get a shot at your dream, to get so close to succeeding, to almost accomplish your desire, and then be denied. That had to be the toughest pill to swallow.

"You know what really bugs me?" he muttered. "I was good. I was catching the passes, running the routes; I had the speed. One day I knew I was in, and the next day, I was gone with the wind."

Chapter 5

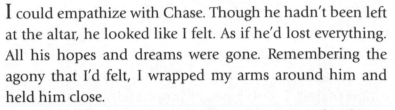

I could empathize with Chase. Though he hadn't been left at the altar, he looked like I felt. As if he'd lost everything. All his hopes and dreams were gone. Remembering the agony that I'd felt, I wrapped my arms around him and held him close.

It was as if my touch hit a release button inside of him. Chase began to sob. Never before had a man cried in my arms. It was almost unbearable seeing him break down, but it also felt good because I wanted to help him. I was determined to lift him up the way he had lifted me.

This world seems so unfair, Lord, I thought. *Why couldn't You give Chase what he wanted so desperately?* It was hard enough for me to get over the Lord not allowing me to have the man I wanted, but it wasn't like I was a perfect Christian. I felt pure shame for all the times Devyn and I had been intimate. It looked as though I was turning into a tramp, which was what my poor mother had become after my dad died. I couldn't be mad at God for not granting me my wish. God sure didn't owe me any favors.

But Chase? He had told me long ago that he was still a virgin and planned to stay that way until he was married. He studied the Word every day. He was practically a walking Bible. He wasn't perfect, but he was the closest thing to Christ I'd ever seen. So why didn't God allow him his heart's desire? It didn't make sense.

"I can't believe God would allow this."

Chase lifted his head off my shoulder and shook his head. "You know what, Zoe? I'm upset, but there is one thing I know. One of my favorite Scriptures says that all things work together for good for those who love Him. I know God's got a reason for taking me through this."

"I can't believe you're saying this—you wanted to be on that team so badly."

"I know," he said with a sniff, "but I just gotta figure out what God's tryin' to say to me. I can't miss it. I don't want to block the blessing. I just gotta praise Him, ask Him for strength and then thank Him." Chase took my hand. "I look at it this way. One guy at training camp got a dislocated shoulder. Another messed up his knee. Even though I got cut from the team, at least I'm healthy."

I couldn't believe the strength Chase already had. Even though he'd broken down, he was still ready to find his blessings.

He said, "Physically, I'm fine."

"You sure are fine," I joked, stroking his muscular arm that seemed bigger than before. "You really worked out in Seattle, didn't you?"

He laughed and I was pleased that I eased his pain a little.

"It's gonna be okay," I assured him. "You're right. God's still in this. He knows what's going on." I wanted to believe the words that I said, but I wasn't sure.

"Yeah," Chase said, eyeing me. "He does."

We hugged each other again, but this time I didn't feel Chase's grief. This time, there was nothing but joy. Chase's situation with the NFL hadn't changed, but he had an inner peace that went beyond his circumstances. Even though he'd been cut from the Seattle team, he knew that he was still a part of God's team.

As we held each other, I prayed that I could have just a little of the light that God had obviously given to Chase.

Chase spent the next two days fasting and lifting God up, thanking the Lord for loving him and saving him. I had never seen anything like it. He became stronger, developing a strength and beauty I'd never witnessed in anyone. I made sure to eat only when Chase wasn't with me, so his fast wouldn't be any harder on him.

While Chase fasted, prayed and read the Bible, I spent my time checking out the classifieds every day. The end of the month was approaching, and I still didn't have a job or a place to live. Now, neither did Chase.

On the third day of Chase's fast, I listened from the hallway as he spent an hour just praising God. As I listened, I waited for Chase to ask God for something—a request to get back on the Seattle Storm or to have another team call him. Anything that would make God work for him. Yet when Chase finished, he had spent the minutes only praising. I went into the living room and sat next to him.

He was breathing heavy, as if he'd just finished working out.

"Why do you spend so much time just thanking the

Lord? I mean, you need to start figuring out what you're gonna do with your life. That's what I've been doing. Checking out want ads, trying to find a new apartment."

"I gotta worship God, Zoe. He can work a miracle anytime. But first He wants to make sure I love Him more than football or anything else in my life. If God wanted to, He could make me a star in the league. But if I can't thank Him when I got nothin', I could easily get off focus when He gives me everything."

I shook my head. "So you still think God is going to work things out for you with the Seattle Storm?"

"I'm not saying He's gonna give me football. Maybe I'll go back to the university and get my degree. I'm only one semester away from finishing. But right now, the only thing I want to do is worship Christ. I've got so much to be thankful for, I just can't stop telling Him about it."

What do you really have to be thankful for was what I wanted to ask him. But I remained silent, keeping my thoughts to myself.

Chase placed his hand on my cheek and stroked my face. "You are so beautiful, Zoe. I feel blessed that God brought you to me."

I smiled. If those sweet words had come from any other guy, I would have thought he was full of it. But I knew Chase was sincere. I was starting to fall in love with him, and not because he worked hard to make me feel that way. The love I felt for Chase was developing slowly and naturally.

Part of me wanted to fight my feelings because, after all, Chase was Devyn's friend. And yet there was another side:

Chase had always made it very clear that he thought I deserved better. Maybe he thought that I deserved him.

I think it was seeing Chase's love for Christ that made me realize I was ready for Chase to love me. It was time for me to tell him.

I turned to face him directly, but the telephone rang. I sighed at first, but as I crossed the room to answer, I felt a sense of relief. The diversion of the phone got me off the hook. Maybe I wasn't ready to tell Chase what I was feeling.

"Hello?" I said into the receiver.

"This is Jerry Sykes from the Seattle Storm. Is Chase Farr in?"

"Yes! Yes. Hold on a second." I stumbled over my words. With the biggest smile on my face, I mouthed to Chase, "It's the team!"

He jumped up and grabbed the phone. I paced the floor and listened for what seemed like an eternity. Then Chase said, "Yes, sir, that would be great. I'll see you Monday. Thank you." He hung up and looked at me with a serious expression I couldn't read.

"Well? What's up? Tell me!"

Suddenly a huge smile lit up his precious face. "They want to sign me, but not on the team. They want to put me on the practice squad."

"What's that?" I frowned, though I wanted to be excited. "If you're on the team, you're on the team, right?"

"The practice squad lines up against the starting guys and practices with them through the week. We're the punching bags. I won't be traveling to away games and I won't suit up for home games. And it's half the salary I would've got if I made the team."

"Hey, it beats the salary you have now, right?" I joked. "Something's better than nothing."

He chuckled. "You're right about that. Seventy grand a year ain't exactly chicken feed."

"What!" I squealed. "How can you not be happy with that kind of money?"

"Oh, I'm very happy. But not just about the salary. I know God's got more for me. You just watch. The practice squad today, twelve touchdowns tomorrow!"

I laughed.

"Man, I gotta get packed. Tomorrow's the last preseason game. I've got to fly up there tomorrow so I'll be ready for the first game of the season, September first, which is next Monday!"

"This is so great!" I flew to him and threw my arms and legs around him. He cupped his hands under me and held me close. "We have to celebrate," I said. "Let's go somewhere special."

"Great idea. A nice restaurant sounds mighty good to me right now! But first," he said as he put me down, "I gotta pray."

He knelt beside the couch. I couldn't believe that the first thing Chase wanted to do was pray, but I joined him. He took both of my hands in his.

"Most precious Father, what an awesome God You are. Thank you for showing me that even in the midst of turmoil and strife, when things are cloudy and I can't see what You're doing, You give me the strength to trust You. Lord, I know You can do great things with this opportunity You've given me. I release all my hopes and desires to You, Lord. Help me to be the best stand-in they've ever seen. And yet, keep me humble. May I not get tired with the hits or try to outshine the Cornerbacks. I want to represent You on the field." He paused and I felt his hands tighten around mine. "And, Lord, thank you for this precious lady You allowed into my life to be my friend and lift me up. Amen."

"Amen!" I said before I opened my eyes and kissed him on the cheek. "Now, where do you want to eat?"

"Anywhere," he exclaimed. "I'm starved!"

"Ouch," I yelled as the crab leg pricked my finger.

"Here, let me do it." Chase reached over and opened my crab leg, then pulled the meat out of the shell with the sea-food fork. He dipped it into the melted butter and held it in front of my mouth. "Here," he said huskily, "let me feed you."

With my eyes glued to his, I opened my mouth and he slipped the crab meat onto my tongue. It was a romantic moment. I felt tingly, and it wasn't because I was eating my favorite food. It was definitely the server who had me heated up.

But although I was truly enjoying the moment, sadness grew inside me. I was thrilled that Chase was getting the chance to live his dream after all. But on the other hand, I hated the fact that he'd be all the way on the other side of the country away from me. Who knew when I would see him again?

"What's wrong?" Chase asked, interrupting my thoughts. "You don't like the food?"

"Oh, I love the crabs." I looked up at him and saw concern in his eyes. "Don't worry. I'm okay."

"No, you're not."

I was amazed that he was so in tune with what was going on inside me. I continued to insist that I was feeling okay.

"I don't care what you say, Zoe. Something is wrong and I'm not going to stop asking you until you tell me what it is."

With every day, every action, every word, I was falling more in love with this guy.

"Okay," I finally admitted. "I'm so happy that you're going back with the Storm, but I'm going to miss you." I lowered my eyes. I didn't want to see his response in his expression.

Chase reached across the table, took my hand and squeezed it, even though both of our fingers were wet and sticky from the food. "I'll only be a phone call away. Anytime you want to talk, you can call me, okay?"

"Are you sure?" I asked, searching his eyes for more.

"Zoe, do you know what I thought was the best thing about being cut from the team and sent home?" I shook my head. "It was knowing I was going to see you."

A smile crossed my face, and I could feel myself blushing. I wondered how much longer I'd be able to hold back my feelings for this wonderful man.

When we returned to the apartment, we settled on the couch. Chase put his arm around me as he flipped the channels, finally settling on the news. I wasn't sure if his gesture was romantic or not, but it felt good as I rested my head on his chest.

All of a sudden, there was a loud crash and we both jumped from the couch.

"What was that?" I asked.

"I don't know. I think something outside."

"It sounded like glass, like a window breaking."

I slipped on my shoes and Chase walked toward the door. I followed him outside. We weren't the first ones to investigate. The parking lot was filled with our neighbors—all standing around a car. My Probe.

The passenger window was shattered; there was glass inside and outside the car. Chase pushed through the crowd, gingerly reaching inside through the sharp edges of the broken glass. He lifted a red brick from the passenger seat. There was a note taped to the brick. He handed the note to me.

I could hear the muttering behind me—nosy neighbors wondering what kind of drama I'd brought to the neighborhood.

"'You best leave my man alone,'" I read softly, not wanting to share my business with everyone. I looked up at Chase. "This is crazy," I exclaimed, trying to keep my voice down. "That Aisha chick has been driving me nuts. Last weekend, she slashed my tires. Now this. I don't know why she thinks I'm still seeing Devyn."

Even though I kept my voice soft, I couldn't stop my body from trembling with anger and frustration.

"Calm down," Chase said, trying to pull me into his arms. "It's okay."

"No, it's not!" I shouted, shaking his arms from me.

Chase grabbed my shoulders. "Let's go inside." He

turned to the crowd around us. "She's all right, y'all. Every-thing's cool."

"This is far from cool," I yelled, finally and completely losing control.

I passed by the men and women, some eyeing me with curiosity, some shaking their heads with pity. As Chase and I walked back toward his apartment, the crowd began to disperse, the night's drama over—at least for them.

But just as we got to Chase's front door, I turned back to the people who were still standing around.

"Did anybody see who threw this?" I asked.

There were a few mumbled noes, though most people kept silent.

I looked through the faces in the crowd. "Surely some-body saw somethin'."

"Zoe, we don't need to get anyone else involved. Let's just go inside and call the police." Chase almost had to push me into the apartment.

"Yeah, right. Like the police are gonna do anything. I couldn't even get through the last time I called them. No, I've got to handle this. I know where she lives."

"How can you be sure Aisha did this or slashed your tires?" he asked as I paced in the living room.

"She came over here the day my tires got cut. She said some crazy things. Obviously Devyn is cheating on her and lying to her. He told her that I still wanted him, and we both know that's not true." I paused, trying to hold back my tears. I didn't want Aisha to win. "I can't take this, Chase. I'm afraid she's gonna do something to me, not just my stuff. I don't feel safe."

"That's why we have to file a report."

"Whatever," I said, continuing my pacing. "But it's not gonna do a bit of good."

Chase picked up the phone, then hesitated before he dropped the receiver back into the cradle. "Listen, I've got an idea." He paused as if his thoughts had not completely formed in his mind. "Why don't you come with me to Seattle? In fact, why don't we leave tonight?"

I stared at him for a moment. "What?" Surely I couldn't have heard right.

"I don't want to leave you here." He began making his argument, waving his hands in the air. "You're still dealing with your grief about the breakup, and now you got this crazy girl scaring you with her stupid stuff. The lease on this place runs out soon, and you haven't found a job or an apartment yet."

"That's true, but I figured I'd just move in with my mother for a while."

"Come on, Zoe. I know you don't want to do that. Think about it. This is a great solution for both of us. Other than the guys on the team, I don't know anybody in Seattle. It'd be nice to come home to a friend every day. Besides, I can keep my eye on you and make sure you don't retaliate against that crazy Aisha."

I laughed, but it was to hide my confusion. Could I really consider his suggestion? He sounded serious.

"It's not like you got a job here." He was continuing his case. "You can find work out there."

"But I don't have . . ."

"Any money?" he said, finishing my sentence for me.

I nodded.

"I get my first check next week. We can stay in hotel rooms until we get settled in."

"I can't just up and go," I argued.

"Why not?"

That was really the same question I was asking myself. I could think of no rational reason to turn down his generous offer. I had no ties to Miami. My mother and brother could manage without me—that was obvious. I hadn't seen them in weeks.

But Seattle, Washington? What on earth would I do there? Then the other side of my brain asked a good question: *What will I do if I stay in Miami?*

Chase picked up on my hesitation. "No matter what you do, you're not going to be able to come up with a good reason not to go with me. So, that's it. We're going to Seattle tonight." He nodded his head strongly, the decision made. "I still want to file the police report, but after we do that, we'll go straight to the airport, purchase your ticket and get on the plane."

"I can't pay for my flight." It was the only argument I could come up with, even though I knew it sounded weak.

"Put it on your credit card. When I get my check, I'll pay for it."

"How do you know there's a flight tonight? You weren't going to leave until the morning."

Chase sighed as if he couldn't believe my weak questions. "I know the schedule from Miami to Seattle. There's a late flight." He looked at his watch. "If you stop arguing with me, we'll make it in plenty of time."

I looked in his eyes, searching for a clue that he didn't really want to do this. "Are you sure about all of this?"

He ran his fingers across my chin. "I want you with me," he said softly. "I want to make sure you're safe, and I want to protect you. Is that okay with you?"

It took a moment for my smile to lighten my face. "Yeah." I got up on my tippy-toes and hugged him tight.

But he broke our embrace a moment later. "Girl, you'd better get packing, and I still have a few things to put together too."

I ran into the bedroom as Chase went into his. I gathered my clothes from the closet, not stopping to fold or put anything in order. I only had a few pieces that would work for the cold place. I'd buy stuff as I needed it.

Seattle! I grinned at the thought. Then I picked up the telephone and called my brother.

"I'm going to Seattle!" I screamed into the phone the moment my brother answered.

"What are you talking about?"

I explained it all to him—Chase's job with the team and his offer for me to go with him. "So, we're leaving tonight. Right now actually."

"Wow! What are you gonna tell Mom?" Alonzo asked. "She's gonna flip, you know."

"I figure I'll call her after I'm settled. That way she can't stop me."

"She'll still lecture you." My brother chuckled.

"Yeah, but better then than now. I'm really not in the mood for it, you know?"

"I hear ya!"

"Hey, come pick up my car, will you? You still have the keys, right?"

"Sure."

"And don't freak out when you see the passenger-side window busted out."

"What?" Alonzo shrieked.

"Long story!"

"Whatever. Maybe it is good that you're going to Seattle."

"You have no idea."

"I gotcha."

"Thanks, Alonzo. I really appreciate this. Just fix the window for me please. I'll call you soon, 'cause Chase is gonna work it out to have my car shipped up there."

My brother paused. I could tell he wanted to say something. Finally, he said, "Hey, are you sure this is such a good idea, taking off with Chase like this? I mean, we've both known him for a long time, and I respect the guy a lot. But it just don't seem right, you up and flyin' across the country with him and all."

I didn't want to tell Alonzo that I'd had the same concerns. "Hey, it's not like I'm gonna live with the guy," I said, trying to console him.

"Yeah, I know." I could tell from his tone that he wasn't convinced.

"I'm gonna be okay."

"I know that too," he assured me. "Don't worry, you have my blessing, Zoe."

I knew Alonzo still had concerns, but I didn't want to focus on that. My brother had given me his blessing and that was enough for me.

"I'll call you when I get there," I told him; then I hung up. I looked at the phone as I laid it back on the nightstand. I couldn't think of a single friend I wanted to say good-bye to. I considered calling Tasha, but after what Keisha told me about my best friend's attitude, I didn't feel much like talking to her. I promised myself that I would call Tasha eventually—I still cared about her.

I dragged my bags into the living room. "What are we going to do with all of this stuff?"

"What stuff?" Chase asked as he lifted a duffel bag onto his shoulder. "The furniture belongs to the landlord, and the other stuff, like the TV and telephones, I'll make arrangements for."

I took a deep breath, sighed and smiled. "Okay. Let's get going."

Chase tossed our bags into the trunk of the car he'd rented when he came back, then drove to the police station. I stayed calm while we filled out the report; my mind was unable to focus on my broken car window. Every brain cell I had was focused on Seattle.

"Now, there's not much we can do right now. We have to catch the person in the act," the desk cop said.

"Yeah, I understand," I said, not really caring. I gave my brother's name, address and phone number for contact information and then eagerly followed Chase back to the car.

As we pulled into the airport parking lot, my pulse started to race. I couldn't believe this was happening. I followed Chase through the ticket line, gave my luggage to the clerk after I purchased my ticket and then followed Chase through the security clearance line. I felt as if I were moving in slow motion, in a daze, as if I were watching myself from a distance.

When we arrived in the waiting area, I sat and stared out the window, watching the airplanes glide down the runway. Here I was, sitting at the airport, about to go cross-country, with a friend—a very good friend. I had entered a make-believe world.

"Good evening, ladies and gentlemen. We're about to begin boarding for Flight three twenty to Seattle. Please have your tickets and IDs available for the attendant. . . ."

"That's our call," Chase said, squeezing my hand. "You ready?"

I stared at him for a moment. I wasn't sure how to answer that question. Though I was excited about going, there were many uncertainties that made me hesitate. I nodded, and he picked up our carry-ons.

I continued moving as if none of this were happening, following behind Chase as he gave our boarding passes to the attendant, then walking to our seats.

I gazed out the small window, watching other airplanes come and go. I was relieved when I heard the door to our airplane close. But still we didn't move.

"Good evening, ladies and gentlemen. This is your pilot, Captain Allen, speaking." I twisted in my seat. "Due to heavy traffic this evening, there is a backup on the runway and air traffic control has asked us to remain at the gate. It shouldn't be too long. We'll try to make up this time in the air and get you to Seattle as soon as possible. In the meantime, if there is anything that the flight attendants can do . . ."

I sighed. There was nothing anyone could do for me except to get me out of Miami. I squirmed in my seat again, not able to find a comfortable spot.

"Are you okay?" Chase stared at me with concern.

I smiled. "Yeah. I just want to get going."

He nodded, then turned back to the American Airlines magazine he'd taken from the seat pocket in front of him.

I turned back to the window. As other planes around us moved, ours sat still. *Maybe this is a sign,* I thought as I tried to loosen my shirt collar, wanting to get some air in the stuffy plane.

As the minutes ticked by, my doubts increased. Was I really doing the right thing? Was this delay God's way of giving me the opportunity to change my mind? I thought about it—I could grab my carry-on, get off the plane and ask the airline to get my luggage out of the cargo bay. Even if they couldn't get my luggage out now, I knew they would arrange to get it to me somehow.

When forty minutes had passed, I decided this was my sign to stay in Miami. I shifted my body so that I could face Chase. I wasn't sure how I was going to explain my decision, but I would just be honest.

"Chase . . ."

He looked up at me.

"Ladies and gentlemen, this is Captain Allen again," his voice crackled over the intercom. "Thank you for your patience. We've finally been cleared for takeoff, and it should be a smooth ride. We'll try to make up some time in the air. Flight attendants, please secure the cabin and prepare for takeoff."

Chase smiled. "You were going to say something?"

I shook my head. The decision had been made for me. I closed my eyes as the plane jerked slightly and then smoothly glided from the gate. Within minutes, we were airborne, flying above the clouds, headed northwest.

When I opened my eyes, Chase was looking at me, smiling.

"What?" I asked.

"I really feel good about this," he said. "I'm so glad you're going with me."

"Yeah, me too," I said, trying to keep my voice from trembling.

"You seem stressed." He frowned. "Are you still worried about the police report? Or is there something else . . . Are you having second thoughts about going to Seattle with me?"

I took a deep breath. "Don't get me wrong, Chase. I'm really excited for you and thankful that you asked me to go. But frankly, I'm just wondering what God has for me. What am I supposed to do in Washington? What am I supposed to do with my life?" I turned away from him, glancing at the window. All I saw was the pitch blackness of night. "Your dream is clear, and it's coming true. I don't even know what my dream is anymore." I shook my head, thinking of all the plans I'd once had for my life. When Chase was silent, I continued. "I mean, I didn't go to college just to find a man, get married and have babies. But the truth be told, once I met Devyn, that was kinda my plan. I don't ever want to think that way again. So I guess I'm searching for what's next for me." I turned back to Chase. "I do know one thing, though. I want my life to be what God wants it to be, you know?"

He took my hand and squeezed it. "You're gonna be just fine."

"I hope you're right." I turned away again and saw tiny droplets of water forming on the oval window. We must have been flying through some moisture. But I still couldn't see anything through the darkness. "At this moment," I mumbled, "my life is just as unclear as that mist."

Chapter 6

With help from Coach Sykes, Chase and I found an apartment after only having to stay in a hotel for two days. It was a two-bedroom in a nice neighborhood and a secure building.

As we stood in the middle of the furnished apartment, checking it out, Chase asked, "Well, what do you think?"

I sighed. "Are you sure you really want us to share an apartment?"

"We did it in Miami."

"Yeah, but we knew that was only temporary."

"Well, this is temporary too. Until you get settled."

I shook my head, unsure of so many things. I didn't know how long it would take for me to find a job and save enough for an apartment. And then, I had my feelings for Chase to contend with. And I knew he also had feelings for me. We were playing with fire.

"Don't worry, Zoe. We'll be fine." He chuckled. "I'll keep you in line."

I hit him playfully on his arm, glad that he always knew the right words to say.

The Seattle Storm had two starting wide receivers and three backups. Chase knew there was no way he'd be able to play that year.

"Then again, you never know," I would say to him whenever he came home a bit down, trying to cheer him up. "Miracles do happen."

As Chase got into the routine for the team, I spent my time making our apartment a home. Even though it was furnished, we needed the little things, like linen and small appliances. I wanted Chase to feel comfortable when he came home each night.

When I wasn't shopping, I spent my time searching the classifieds, determined to find my own way. As the days went by and nothing seemed to be coming my way, I had to fight to keep my sadness away from Chase. He had done too much for me—I couldn't now bring him down with my problems.

But while nothing seemed to be going my way, things were changing for Chase.

During practice on the day before their last preseason game, things began falling apart for the team. Steven Dunn, one of the backup receivers, was injured. Then Darryl Williams, another backup, began dropping balls. Coach Sykes immediately pulled him from the lineup.

"Only Michael Powell is left," Chase said excitedly when he came home that night.

The next day, Chase and I watched the first game of the season from our apartment. We sat in stunned amazement, when with only two minutes into the game, Calvin Baker, the starting receiver, misread his play and missed his catch, which resulted in an interception. The ball was run back for a touchdown—for the opposing team.

"That guy's in trouble," Chase muttered, referring to Calvin.

Chase was right. But it wasn't only Calvin who was in trouble. By halftime, the Storm was down, 21–0.

"I'm gonna take a quick shower," Chase mumbled, shaking his head and rising from the couch. I watched as he lumbered into the bathroom. Even though he was just on the practice squad, I knew it bothered him to see his team getting trounced so badly.

After watching part of the halftime show, I went into the kitchen and made two sandwiches. I hoped that I could cheer up Chase with some food.

By the time I returned to the living room, the second half was starting. I sat, took a bite of my sandwich and watched as the opposing punter kicked the ball, sailing it far down the field. It looked like the Storm was going to begin deep in their territory.

But as the ball began its descent, two receivers tried to make the play, finally bumping into each other and fumbling the ball.

"Chase," I yelled. "Come quick! You've got to see this!" I sat on the edge of the couch. When Chase didn't come out, I figured he couldn't hear me over the shower, so I ran to the bathroom door and banged on it. "You're not gonna believe the play I just saw, Chase. Hurry up so you can see the replay."

Suddenly the door opened and Chase stood there, with only a towel wrapped around his waist. The man was unbelievably fine. I forgot all about the replay as my hands roamed over his muscular chest, and then my lips followed. His chest was as muscular as any woman could ever desire. His fingers combed through my hair and he pulled me closer. He lowered his lips, almost meeting mine, and I blinked.

Reality came crashing in. I was still standing in front of the closed door, breathing heavily at the scene that I'd created in my mind. The whole thing had been pure fantasy.

I wished that the seduction had not been a dream. But this wasn't the kind of relationship we had, and I needed to hold off on what I thought I wanted until the time was right.

While I stood catching my breath, the bathroom door opened, for real this time. Chase stood in front of me, completely dressed in jeans and a T-shirt, rubbing a towel over his wet hair. "What is it, Zoe?"

I grabbed his arm and pulled him into the living room to the television. "Look at this."

He watched the replay in amazement. The announcers found it so amusing they showed it several times in slow motion, followed by a shot of the coach reaming the two receivers.

"Dang, that's a trip. I can't believe this." Chase looked at me. "Zoe, do you know what this means?" He paused as if he couldn't believe what he was about to say. "I might be the third man on Monday."

"Do you think you can handle it?" I asked with a grin.

"Watch me! I've worked hard for this, and you know it. If I get an opportunity, you better believe I'm gonna bust it wide open," he exclaimed, bouncing onto the couch. "Sometimes you only get one chance for your dream."

Suddenly he jumped up and threw his arms around me. He lifted me from the floor and swung me around.

I giggled. I'd never seem him so excited. I was excited too, but not just because of his opportunity. His strong arms felt so good around me. The embrace was incredible. I couldn't help but be all into him. But I knew I couldn't let him know it. Not yet.

"What?" he said as he put me down and looked into my face. I hadn't noticed that my grin was gone.

"Nothing. I'm happy for you."

He stroked my cheek. "I'm really glad you're in my corner."

Chase released me from his embrace. "I've got to get prayed up." I watched him strut down the hall to his bedroom. That man had it going on, in more ways than one!

"I don't know why you want me to go to this luncheon thing tomorrow," I complained as I dug through my closet trying to find *something* appropriate to wear.

"It's the first function of the season. All the wives, fiancées, girlfriends and significant others are invited."

I don't fit into any of those categories, I thought as I lifted two pantsuits from my closet and held them side by side.

"Besides," Chase continued, "since you don't have any friends out here, I thought this would be a great place for you to make some new acquaintances."

"Oh, goody," I groaned, remembering how Tasha had talked about me to my hairdresser. She was supposed to be my best friend, so I truly didn't care about having a relationship with another female.

"What's wrong?" Chase asked, touching my shoulder to get my attention.

I stopped fidgeting and looked at him. "I'm not sure I want to meet any of the players' wives, Chase."

"Why not?" He frowned.

"You don't understand women." I sighed. "Sometimes they're for you; other times they're against you. One day they like you; the next day, they're jealous. Quite frankly, I can't figure women out."

Chase laughed, obviously thinking I'd made a great joke.

I slumped onto my bed. I hadn't met any of the NFL wives, but I was sure the luncheon would be filled with rich, snooty, arrogant women. What would they think of me? What could I talk about? What would I possibly have in common with them? I didn't care about babies, bottles, curtains, drapes or china. I didn't have the big diamonds, fancy cars and huge houses they all did. I just wouldn't fit in.

And I never expected to fit in. I didn't know who I was yet, but I knew I didn't want to be like what I imagined the NFL wives to be. I wanted a job, regardless of the feelings I was having for Chase. Even if things worked out for us, and his career took off the way he wanted it to, I'd never want to stay at home and sit on my rump. The "shop till you drop" mentality just wasn't me. "How will I get there?" I asked, knowing we just had one rental car.

Quickly he responded, "I'ma get scooped up. You can drive the car. We'll have yours shipped next week."

It took him a few more minutes, but Chase finally convinced me to go.

"Come on, do it for me." Those were the words that finally did me in.

As I drove to the restaurant the following day, I tried to talk myself into believing that I was going to have a good time.

But I couldn't do it. I was sure that I knew what it would be like. There was no way I could have a good time. But I was doing this for Chase.

I didn't feel any better when I slowed in front of the restaurant and the valet helped me from the car. I held my breath as I entered one of Seattle's most exclusive restaurants. I paused in the doorway and surveyed the place.

Tuxedoed waiters scurried around, balancing champagne and cocktails on silver trays. The tables were covered with white linen and lit by tiny candles in crystal holders. Ladies dressed in expensive clothes chatted in small clusters throughout the room. I glanced down at my plain old green dress and realized how dreadfully out of place I looked.

A petite brown-skinned girl in a simple skirt and blouse came up and flashed a pleasant smile. "Hi. I'm Shay Smith," she said.

"Zoe Clarke."

"Nice to meet you." She lowered her voice to a whisper. "Uh-oh. Here comes the crew." I followed her gaze and saw three women strutting toward us. They looked exactly like I'd expected snobby NFL wives to look, right down to their perfectly styled hair. "I've been avoiding them all day," Shay said.

"What do you mean?" I questioned.

"You'll see." She giggled.

"Hello," one of the ladies said with a sugary voice. "And whose wives are you?"

I couldn't speak for Shay, but I said, "I'm not anyone's wife."

"Fiancée?" the second woman asked.

Shay and I shook our heads.

The third woman peered at us like we were trespassers probably there to steal the restaurant's silverware. "Well, who *are* you with, girls?"

"I'm a good friend of Chase Farr's," I said.

"Who?" the second lady asked, one eyebrow raised.

The first woman leaned closer to the other two and whispered loudly enough for Shay and me to hear: "He's on the practice squad."

"Oh," the ladies chorused.

The three of them looked around as if it were beneath their dignity to even be seen talking to us.

"Zoe," Shay said with a playful grin, "allow me to introduce you to these fine ladies." She pointed to the first woman who had spoken to us. "This is Mrs. Spalding."

I knew all about superstar running back Bryce Spalding. He'd rushed for over a thousand yards the last two seasons.

"And this," Shay said, nodding toward woman number two, "is Mrs. Peterson." Defensive lineman Ricky Peterson was another superstar. That guy never missed a beat. You could count on him to sack the quarterback and recover a forced fumble every game. "He came from an HBC, you know," Shay added, knowing I would recognize the lingo for a historically black college.

Shay then introduced me to Mrs. Simmons. Defensive back Dre Simmons played baseball in the off season, and he'd signed a $20 million contract with the Storm that year. I knew all this because Chase had schooled me on the team during the past week.

While Shay introduced me, none of the ladies made eye

contact or even acknowledged that Shay was talking to them. Their eyes flitted around the room as if searching for other women to be with—besides us.

Finally, Mrs. Simmons said, "Well, you ladies enjoy your time here. It's a seventeen-week season, but some people's stay here is significantly shorter than others." They disappeared into the crowd without even a backward glance.

I was right about this luncheon, I thought, irritated by their attitude. How dare they treat us like dirt just because we weren't married to professional football players? Then again, I was glad they showed their true colors right away. I would never want to make friends with such people.

I turned to Shay. She looked ready to cry.

"Why are you lettin' those old goats get to you?" I asked.

"Because I really do want them to like me."

"Why do you care?"

Shay sniffed. "When I came here last year to visit, my man was on the bench. His name is Byron Johnson by the way. He's getting a new jersey number. This year, he's getting some playing time. He's sure he's going to be the starter soon. But he hasn't been getting any respect around here. If those ladies are treating me like a nobody, maybe Byron isn't doing as well as he's been telling me."

"Don't be so gloomy," a gentle voice from behind us said. Shay and I turned around. "Hi, I'm Fawn Pierce, Frankie's wife."

Wearing a blue suit, with sparkles blaring in my face, she was dressed as elegantly as many of the other women, but she looked different immediately. The way she smiled and looked at us let me know that she wasn't like the other wives I'd just met, although she had every right to be snooty. Her husband, Frankie Pierce, was the starting wide receiver, the only one who hadn't been injured, cut or benched. He'd been in the league for eight years, and a starter for six. He was a phenomenal athlete, and most people said he still hadn't come into his full potential.

"You can't let those biddies get to you," Fawn began, and waved her hand in the air. "They treat everybody like that. But what you need to know is that not all players' wives are that cold."

"It doesn't even make sense for them to talk to people the way they do."

"Well, I'm not making excuses for them, but a lot of fiancées and girlfriends never become wives. They come and go like they're moving through a revolving door. It's not that we have to be careful who we talk to, but to be honest, it's hard to remember the names. And the fact is, you two are girlfriends—"

"I'm nobody's girlfriend," I said, cutting her off. "I'm just a good friend."

"Of whose?" she probed.

"Chase Farr."

"Chase? Oh, Frankie likes him. Ever since camp he's been talking about Chase. He's always telling me what a great guy he is, and how excited he is about the possibility of Chase getting playing time soon."

"Really?" I said.

"Oh, yes," Fawn confirmed. "You know, there aren't very many Christians on this team."

"You're Christians too?" Shay asked.

Fawn smiled. "Well, I can see the three of us are going to get to know each other very well." Fawn took our elbows. "Why don't y'all sit with me?"

After the luncheon, I used the time to run errands: I picked up clothes from the dry cleaners and purchased toiletries from Wal-Mart. When I returned to our apartment, Chase was waiting for me.

"How was the luncheon?"

I kicked off my shoes. "It turned out to be okay," I admitted.

He smiled. "Good," he said in an "I told you so" tone. "You must have made some friends."

"I wouldn't go that far, but there were a couple of women who seemed pretty nice."

Chase leaned back on the couch as if he had just scored the winning touchdown in a football game. "I'm glad to hear that." He paused. "'Cause we've been invited to go to dinner at one of the players' homes tonight."

I sighed. My day hadn't been that good. "Do we have to go? I did the social stuff all day."

Chase took my hand. "I'd really like to. It's one of the wide receivers."

I flopped down on the couch. "I'd much rather stay here with you. Just kick back, hear about your day and do nothing. Is that okay?"

That might have sounded selfish, but I just could not muster up the energy to accept the dinner invitation. Chase could have pouted about my decision, but even in his reluctance, he was supportive. I was falling deep for this guy.

Though Chase's face showed his disappointment, he still said, "That's cool. I'll just call and cancel."

"Thanks," I said with a relieved sigh. I felt a bit selfish since I could tell that Chase really wanted to go to this dinner. But I had done all the socializing I could do for him in one day. I would find a way to make it up to him.

As Chase walked to the phone, I noticed a newspaper sitting on the coffee table. The sports page was on top, and Chase's picture was on the front page.

"Hey, what's this?" I asked, picking it up. A quick skim told me the great news. "You're starting this weekend!"

Chase rushed back into the room, the phone call forgotten. "I haven't read the whole article yet, but I get the impression this sportswriter doesn't think I have the talent."

"No way." I patted the couch. "Come on over here, and we'll read it together."

As he sat down, I once again started to imagine things that weren't happening. In my mind, I eased up to him and snatched the paper from his hand, threw it to the floor and kissed him from his forehead to his luscious lips.

I regained control of my desires and tried to concentrate on the article. But then I noticed him smiling at me.

I wondered what was on his mind. For years, I had told Chase we could be nothing more than friends. After all, I was his best friend's girl. But that was no longer true. He was available and so was I. And from what I saw, he wouldn't be available for long. Someone would want to make him hers. I knew I wanted to be the one who won him over.

But could I? I was sure that he'd gotten used to the idea of just being friends with me. But I longed to tell him everything that had been building in my heart.

Would it matter, though? Would he care? Would he want to go beyond what we had now? Could we be an item? Would he wrap his strong, muscular arms around me and kiss my fears away? I just didn't know.

So I said nothing. Instead, I followed along as Chase read the article out loud. But my thoughts weren't with him. My mind was still on all that I wanted to happen between us. I didn't know which way I would eventually go. My doubts were as hazy as a cloud.

Chapter 7

"Touchdown!" I heard a man in the stands behind me holler.

"A solid catch by Chase Farr," came over the intercom.

I sprang to my feet and screamed. Chase had done it! He had made his starting debut a success. That eighty-yard catch was his third reception for a touchdown in this game.

With under a minute left in the fourth quarter, it looked like the Seattle Storm would win their first game of the season. And Chase was responsible for most of the action.

My new friend Shay Smith gave me a high five as we sat back down.

"Way to go!" she shouted as we settled back into our seats.

I laughed because she'd said that as if I had caught the ball. But I knew she was excited for me, just as I had been when her beau caught the only other touchdown in the game. We were two proud women.

Several other folks sitting in the players' section gave us thumbs-up. We even received smiles from the three wives who had been so rude to us at the luncheon.

When the game clock ran out, we were all standing on our feet and cheering as the final score gave the Storm their first win. With a throat sore from screaming, I rushed to the locker room, wanting to be the first to congratulate my friend.

But when Chase sauntered out of the locker room, almost thirty minutes later, I couldn't get anywhere near him. Reporters and fans swarmed around him, so I stood back and smiled. Chase deserved this.

As the crowd began to disperse, I moved closer, wanting to get my turn at Chase. Just as I got close, a voluptuous chick, with hair weaved down to her butt and wearing the tightest black miniskirt I'd ever seen, pranced up to Chase. Wordlessly, she took a piece of paper out of her low-cut blouse and shoved it into his hand.

I squeezed between her and Chase.

"Hey, baby, great game. You ready to go?" I planted a kiss on his cheek.

"Excuse me, girl, but we were talking," the floozy said, swinging her hair into my face.

Chase took my hand. "She's with me," he said. "I don't think I'll be needing this." He graciously handed her the piece of paper. Then he placed his arm around my waist and walked me out of the dome.

Although we were only steps away from his car, it still took almost an hour to get there. Players, coaches, reporters, and fans constantly stopped us, wanting to offer their congratulations or to get an autograph. It didn't bother me. Chase had waited a long time for this. It was his time to sparkle.

Still, I was eager to be alone with him. I knew today that I could no longer hide what I was feeling. He was definitely the total package—the type of man I wanted to spend my life with. Even though I'd known this for several weeks, today all of my emotions seemed to converge.

I stood back and watched him with the fans. His dream had emerged, but that wasn't what made him so attractive. It was the glow that he wore, not from his football victory, but from the favor he had from God that allowed those dreams to come true. God was smiling down on Chase because he never doubted what God could do.

Granted, there were several more games to be played before Chase could be considered a true player in this league. But this amazing game—with almost three hundred receiving yards, some tremendous catches that others would have dropped and one snatch from a cornerback that probably would've been an interception—showed that Chase Farr was on his way to stardom.

By the time we got to the car, I was ready to show my own appreciation. I gave him an enormous hug. When I tried to pull back, he held me close and I relented. Neither one of us wanted to let go.

Keeping his arms around me, Chase whispered, "Today was a great day for me. But a lot of what I needed to succeed was given to me when I glanced into the stands and saw your gorgeous face smiling at me. I was in the zone."

I held my breath as he held me closer.

"I love you, Zoe," he whispered into my ear.

It only took a moment for our lips to meet. It was a soft, sweet, innocent kiss, filled with passion that we'd both kept hidden away.

He loved me, and I loved him. This felt so different from anything I'd ever experienced. And this wasn't the beginning stages of a budding romance. This was full, blossoming love.

When he finally leaned back, tears slid down my face. I was overcome by the love I could feel from him.

"Baby, don't cry," he said.

"How can I not?" I replied as more tears flowed. "Just a few weeks ago I thought love was over for me. But God is so good. He knew what He was doing when He let Devyn leave me. I'm so happy right now." I took his hand in mine and kissed his palm. "I love you too, Chase, and you're a blessing I don't deserve."

He smiled at me. "We all deserve God's blessings."

I shook my head. "Look at my history with Devyn. That wasn't how God expects dating to be." I paused and stroked Chase's precious face. "Yet, despite how messed up I am, God gave me a tremendous blessing. I am so full of love for both you and God right now."

Chase's soft dark brown eyes caressed me with his love. The kind of love every girl longs to experience. The kind of love every girl expects to have only once in a lifetime. And I knew that this was the true kind of love that God wanted me to experience.

Over the next two weeks, Chase continued to play amazing football. It was a whirlwind of success, with fans cheering, the press calling, and through it all, Chase loving me. I was the most blessed woman in the world.

And even though Chase was very affectionate with me in

public, we made no formal announcement about our relationship. So, I wasn't very surprised when a lady from the public-relations department for the Seattle Storm called me for an interview. I had heard that players' significant others never work in the front office. Rightfully so, I guess. But what would happen now? When I'd applied for the job, Chase and I were just friends. Now we were much more than that. I was nervous. If they knew Chase and I were involved, surely I wouldn't get the job. And I really wanted it. I was tired of letting him make our way.

"You're going to be terrific, sweetheart," Chase said to me when I told him my concerns. "They are gonna want you because you're good. So what if they find out. I want the whole world to know that you're my woman!"

By the time I sat down with Kelly Wallace, I felt better. And when she asked me that first question, I knew I'd be all right. The questions were simple, easygoing: How did I like Seattle? What were the major differences between Seattle and Miami? I was relieved that she kept the interview to what I wanted to do; I wouldn't have felt too comfortable talking about my personal life.

"So, what are you doing here in Seattle?" Kelly asked.

I sighed. "I'm still searching for the perfect job."

"What are you interested in doing?"

"Actually, I have a degree in public relations and I really hope to work in the field."

Kelly snapped her notepad shut. "You know what, Zoe? I think I might have an opportunity for you. We don't have anything open in that department here, but . . ."

In minutes, she gave me the details and set me up for an interview with Blanche Wright, a sharp-tongued Bo Derek look-alike. Blanche was a private party-planner who gave some of the hottest shindigs in Seattle.

That same day, I went to Blanche's work address, and she and I were only ten minutes into my interview when Blanche said, "Zoe, I like your style. You're hired."

I wanted to jump up and kiss her. But instead, I remained in one of the two leather chairs in front of her desk. "Thank you, Blanche. I'll do a good job for you."

"You'll get paid by the job," Blanche explained. "But you don't have to worry. There is plenty of work."

This job would be better for me than working for the Storm anyway, I thought. *I can still do what I love, and Chase and I won't have to keep our relationship a secret.*

The first weekend after I started, I helped Blanche do the grand opening for a chic local restaurant. For just that project, I received $1,200. Next, we dedicated a library, and I got $800. I was ecstatic.

I was even more excited when Blanche called me into her office and told me that we would be doing the governor's ball.

"You'll make three grand for this," Blanche said nonchalantly.

"Three thousand dollars?" I wanted to make sure that she hadn't made a mistake.

Blanche grinned. "Don't worry, honey. You'll earn every penny."

I didn't care how hard I had to work. At that rate, I'd soon be making more money than Chase!

A few weeks later, I was dressing for the governor's ball in a body-fitting silver gown that was both elegant and sexy. I waited in the living room for Chase to come out of his bedroom. Not only was he going to be my escort, but he was also a guest speaker.

I turned when I heard his footsteps. I whistled and he grinned.

"You look good," I said, licking my lips playfully.

He bowed slightly and said, "You don't look bad yourself."

I twirled, knowing that I looked good. "You like?"

He nodded.

I loved the way he looked at me.

A limousine took us to the hotel, and when we arrived, the entryway was filled with other limousines and cars dropping off guests. It was going to be an elegant affair, with politicians and other dignitaries mixing with many of the athletes from the Storm and the other Seattle teams. At the entryway to the ballroom, I paused, taking in the sight of the white-and-gold decorated room.

Chase pointed to the ice sculpture of a wave sitting in the center of the buffet table. "That is gorgeous."

We walked closer to the table. "Do you like it?" I said. "I figured with all the excitement about the Storm, I'd get a sculpture with the team's logo."

"Sweet!" He looked around the room. "Did you do all this?"

I nodded. "A lot of the decorations were my idea. Working with Blanche is great. She's allowing me to blend my personal taste with her flair. It's a cool mix."

"Come here," Chase said in a romantic tone, putting his arm around my waist. "There's something I forgot to tell you." He placed his lips near my ear. "The sculpture is beautiful," he whispered, "but it doesn't have anything on you. Baby, you got it goin' on. You look great."

I smiled, inside and out. "You look mighty fine too," I said. "You could be a model."

I floated through the evening, mixing with the guests and making sure that everything proceeded smoothly. I even had the chance to pause and listen when Chase spoke.

He didn't want me to hear his speech ahead of time. The only thing I knew was its title, "Staying Afloat When the Waters Are Raging." He did a fantastic job with his address. It was basically the story of how he made it to the NFL, and it was so inspirational.

As I watched him onstage, I had another fantasy. I imagined running up to him, pushing the mike away and kissing him like he'd never been kissed before.

I shook my head. *What is wrong with me? Oh, how I want that man!*

After his speech, Chase was flooded by guests wanting to offer their congratulations, wanting to tell him how excited they were to have him with the Storm.

I stood to the side, wanting to watch him as he stood in his glory.

"You know what? *You* are the Storm!" one man exclaimed.

Others around Chase agreed, but he didn't. Chase shook his head. "No, this is definitely a team effort."

I smiled with pride. There was no denying that Chase had made the difference on that team. Since he joined, the offense was doing better than ever, averaging thirty points a game. They had won four games in a row.

"Chase, you can be modest if you want to," the man continued. "But come on, tell us your secret."

Chase lowered his head, just a bit. "There's no secret. Any success I have is due to my Lord and Savior, Jesus Christ. Every victory I help the team achieve comes from the Lord."

At those words, I walked to the back of the ballroom. I was sure that Blanche was looking for me and I had heard enough. Those words were the reason why I was so in love with that man.

October 13th was the seventh game of the season and Chase went off by himself—again. He was taking our relationship slowly, and I knew God was guiding his steps. That should have been enough for me. But I longed for things to go a little faster.

Still, I was excited about the game and made plans for Shay and Fawn to come over to our apartment to watch the game on TV. I was grateful for the support and friendship of Shay and Fawn. Over the weeks, we'd become closer.

"I don't know why I'm so nervous about this game," I said as I placed a bowl of potato chips on the table.

"Girl, you don't have a thing to be nervous about." Shay laughed. "Your man is a star! And next week you don't have to be stressed because it's a bye week."

I laughed with Shay, but I still shook inside. I realized that any game could be Chase's last. There was always the possibility that he could have a bad day or get injured.

"Can the winning streak continue?" the announcer asked as I turned up the TV's volume just minutes before the game was to begin. "Since Chase Farr got on the field, the Seattle Storm have been unbeatable. But is there any reason to believe that their luck will continue? Is this guy really a diamond in the rough? Before this season, no one had ever heard of this bench rider from the University of Miami. But we sure have heard of him now."

The announcer's words made me feel even more uneasy. Shay and Fawn chatted as I watched the Storm, then San Diego, taking the field. I said a quick, quiet prayer as the captains did the coin toss and sighed when San Diego got the ball first.

That's not a good sign, I thought.

I was right.

During the first three quarters, Chase dropped two passes and fumbled one sure catch, which was picked up by San Diego and run back for a touchdown. I saw the dejection in Chase's face when a camera zoomed in for a close-up of him. All I wanted to do was reach through the television and put my arms around him.

"It looks like the honeymoon is over for Chase Farr," the announcer said. It almost sounded as if he were chuckling, enjoying Chase's demise.

It was all I could do to hold back my tears.

Fawn noticed my anguish. "Oh, come on, Zoe. It's not that serious. This is just one game."

Her words released my floodgates. Tears started to flow.

Shay put her arm around me and handed me a tissue. "You can't go crying just 'cause your guy's not doing well."

"It's not the stupid game," I blubbered. "I just want him so bad, and I don't know what to do."

"You've already got him, girl," Fawn said.

"But I want us to be . . . together." I sniffed into the tissue.

"You mean physically?" Shay asked as if she were surprised.

"Yeah." I pointed to the screen. "Look at him. He's so fine! I think about being with him all the time!"

"I know what you mean, girl," Shay said, shaking her head. "I think about being with Byron all the time. Well, at least I used to." Shay looked down at her finger and at the huge rock on it, which her guy had just given her last week. "Then I started praying about it, and God let me know that our time would be coming soon. So now, I think about other things in our relationship, and now it doesn't bother me so much."

Through my tears, I sighed with relief. I wasn't sure what Shay and Fawn would think once I said that I wanted to be with Chase. In the past, I'd known people who were Christians, and many times, I found them to be judgmental. So, I was glad to know that Shay had experienced the same feelings I had.

It was also good to know that I could be real with Shay and Fawn.

"But don't you think he needs . . . you know, to be intimate?"

"You are so naive, Zoe," Fawn said. "Do you really

believe a guy needs to have it? That if you don't give it up, he's gonna go out there and sleep with the first thing that walks his way?"

I hadn't said any of that, but I was amazed that Fawn knew exactly what I'd been thinking. I knew it was only a matter of time before some woman caught Chase's eye. And, with her, he might suddenly decide not to wait.

I said, "Well, that's true of most of the guys I've ever known."

Shay laughed.

"I mean, I'm sure he's at least thinking about it. He is a man, after all. You know what I'm saying?" I giggled, wiping my tears away.

Fawn stared at Shay and me. "Personally, I don't think that's funny." She crossed her arms in front of her. "You need to get your mind off that." She paused. "One of the reasons you might be thinking a lot about being with Chase is because you're living here with him. The best thing for you to do is to stop living together."

I forgot all about my tears and I looked at her with wide eyes.

"It was one thing when you and Chase were just friends," Fawn continued. "But now that you guys are dating, this sort of arrangement is shacking."

"How can it be shacking when my room is clear on the other side of the apartment?" I argued.

"You're still in the same house. You said you think about being with Chase all the time. If you keep this up, you're going to end up having sex with him. The temptation is not going to go away."

I shook my head. "We're fine—"

"This will put a strain on your relationship," Fawn interrupted me. "I know that's not what he wants."

"How do *you* know what he wants?" My face grew hot.

"Because when he came over for dinner a few nights ago, Chase told Frankie that he wasn't interested in anyone. Frankly, I was quite surprised when you said you two were now dating."

Inside, my heart pounded, but I tried to keep cool. "Maybe he just told your husband that because he didn't want our relationship out there. We agreed to keep it secret."

"So, why did you tell us?" Fawn snapped back.

"'Cause I thought we were friends. Mistakenly, I thought we could talk like that."

"I want to be your friend, Zoe," Fawn said. "But I have to be honest. I have to intervene when I see two Christian friends about to fall. It doesn't make sense for you to put Chase in a situation that will compromise all that he's done. I truly hope that he remains a virgin. There aren't too many out there."

I swallowed. I had never told Fawn or Shay that Chase was a virgin. So, I knew that he had told Fawn's husband everything.

"And from what you told me about your relationship with that guy who left you at the altar," Fawn continued her case, "you're not a virgin. So, don't try to mess up someone who is."

I was angry now. And hurt. And I wanted to hurt Fawn back. "I think you're just jealous 'cause you don't get enough, even though you're married."

"Hey, y'all, calm down," Shay said, standing up between us as if she were going to have to be a referee. "Let's get some love up in here."

I stared at Shay, but I wasn't mad at her. She was cool, though I knew she didn't understand where I was coming from. She and Byron were getting married. All they had to do was set a date. They had a level of commitment that was much higher than what Chase and I shared.

But Fawn! How dare she look down on me? She was married. She couldn't possibly understand what I was feeling, wanting to be with my man but being weighed down by knowing that wasn't how God wanted it to be.

If I'd learned anything in my relationship with Devyn, it was that doing things my way wasn't right. Now I was learning that doing things God's way was really hard. All I needed was a little help and I thought I would get it from my friends. But Fawn was definitely not helping with her high-and-mighty talk.

"Hey, guys, look!" Shay pointed to the TV.

While we were arguing, the Storm had made a comeback.

"This is quite a turnaround," the announcer said. "But I don't think the Storm can pull it out."

The score flashed on the screen: San Diego 21, Seattle 14.

The announcer continued: "There's only one minute left and San Diego has the ball deep in Seattle territory."

Silently, the three of us settled on the edge of the couch. We watched the San Diego quarterback roll back and toss the ball to one of his running backs. But a moment later, a defensive back knocked the ball from his hands, giving the Storm possession.

We stood and cheered.

"There's still plenty of time," I said, clasping my hands together.

"It was a good play, but with only forty seconds left, I think the Storm's good luck has run out," the announcer said as if he were responding to me.

I shook as the Storm huddled and then lined up. The quarterback rolled back and threw the ball to Frankie. The ball wobbled in his hands for a second and then dropped to the ground.

Fawn groaned.

Ten seconds had been wasted and I realized the Storm had no time-outs left. Again, our quarterback dropped back, and this time, he threw the ball to Chase. He caught it on the thirty-six yard line and ran toward the end zone.

Shay and Fawn and I jumped up and screamed at the TV.

"Run, Chase! Run, baby!" I yelled.

When Chase scored, running all the way to the end zone untouched, our screams rattled walls.

We screamed and laughed and hugged.

"You can't tell me that brother don't deserve some lovin' when he gets home," I said. Instantly, the joy and excitement evaporated from the room.

Fawn dropped her arms from around me. "I'm gonna say one thing to you, girl, and then I'm gonna go." Fawn paused. "I think you need to pack your stuff and leave before that brother gets home."

I couldn't believe what Fawn was saying. But before I could say a word, she continued. "The reason that man's got the talent he does is because he's being blessed by God.

And your desires may cause him to stumble. His relationship with God could be altered because of you."

I stood, speechless. How could this woman be saying such things to me?

"Now, I'm not saying this to be mean or cruel," Fawn went on, "so don't look at me like I'm something horrible. We Christians usually don't stand up for what's right when others come and destroy our walk with Christ. We just sit back and allow it to happen. But the Bible says we're supposed to bear one another's burdens, and that means we've got to get involved, even get in each other's faces when we have to."

I was too angry to speak. This was exactly the kind of thing I'd tried to explain to Chase when he encouraged me to make new friends. I knew I was headed for trouble with females.

"Zoe, I'm telling you what I believe God wants me to say. If you really care about Chase, you can't go bringing him down. Which is better—passion that will make him feel good for one night, or being able to smile when he gets to heaven because he knows he honored God?"

Finally, words came to my lips. "Get out of my face, Fawn. And get out of my house."

"*Your* house?" she asked. Without waiting for an answer, she grabbed her purse and strutted out the door. I slammed it as hard as I could behind her.

I turned. Shay was sitting quietly on the couch. By the time I joined her, her silent look of concern had melted my anger, and all I felt was confusion. "Do you think she's right, Shay?" I asked softly.

"What do you think?"

"I don't know."

"You sounded pretty sure of yourself a few minutes ago."

I shook my head. "I wasn't, but I couldn't let Fawn know I thought she might be right." My head fell into my hands. "But Fawn's right. I've got to get out of here!" I got up, raced to my room and began throwing clothes into my suitcases. "I can't make Chase stumble. I can't be his downfall." I kept saying those words over and over.

Shay stood in the doorway. "Couldn't you just put your thoughts about sex out of your mind for a little while?"

I stopped and looked up at her. "If I could, I would. But it's like a battle within me, and the flesh is winning. I feel things for Chase that I *never* felt for Devyn. We talk and we bond. I know he loves me."

I sat on the bed and lowered my head. "Chase is growing in his walk with God, Shay, and my relationship with the Lord is at a standstill."

Shay came over and sat next to me. "Well, you can do something about that, Zoe."

"I don't know what. I don't even know if I want to grow. I feel like I'm frozen in my stance, like a solid block of ice."

Chapter 8

"Please let me in, Zoe," Chase said through the hotel room door. He sounded sweet and desperate at the same time. "I know you're in there."

I wondered how he had found me. I'd left the apartment before he came home and the only thing my note said was that I had to get away. But then, I'd called Shay. She'd made me promise to let her know that I was okay.

Obviously that was my mistake. I'd have to straighten her out later.

"Zoe, I have to talk to you," Chase continued pleading.

I felt bad for him, but there was really nothing to be said. This was the only way I knew how to protect him—from me.

"If you don't let me in, I'm sure I can get the key from downstairs." His tone was growing more insistent.

With a deep sigh, I threw on my bathrobe and opened the door. Chase stood in the hallway, snow scattered over his coat and hair. His body still trembled from the chill, and he stared at me for a moment.

Then he threw his arms around me and squeezed me tight. His coat was wet and cold, but his embrace made me feel warm inside.

I had to get away. This didn't help keep away my desire to be physical with him. And knowing how much Chase cared about me wasn't making it any easier.

With great emotional effort, I pushed him away. "Chase, you gotta go. If you need to talk, we can do it over the phone. But I can't be with you."

"Why not?" His voice cracked with sorrow. "I don't understand."

"Chase, I . . . I'm no good for you."

In one swift movement, Chase entered my hotel room and closed the door. He took off his coat and then took my hand. He led me to the fireplace, where he sat in the chair across from me. I watched him rub his fingers in front of the fire.

Staring into the flames, Chase whispered, "Shay told me what happened."

I knew my friend had betrayed me, but something in my heart told me that I should be thanking her, rather than being angry.

Chase continued to speak. "Believe me, I know it's difficult not to take our relationship any further. I've wanted you for four years, Zoe, so maybe it's easier for me to subdue my feelings because I've been putting them off for so long."

My heart began to beat faster.

"Sometimes I see you walking around the house wearing just a T-shirt. Your hips, them thighs. Hey, I'm all man, baby. It gets harder to resist you every day." He turned and looked into my eyes. "But I don't know that walking away from the relationship is better. I've been praying for us for so long. We can be strong together; I know we can. I love you, Zoe."

I wanted to get up, sit in his lap and hug him tight. But I didn't want to destroy the moment. This time, what I felt for Chase wasn't a physical joy, but a spiritual high. He understood me. I wasn't alone. Chase was wrestling with the same desires I had.

"I love you too," I said.

"You coming back to the apartment, then?" he asked, his eyes full of hope.

"Not yet," I replied against every desire inside me. "I'm gonna stay here tonight and think."

I could see the disappointment in his face.

"Chase, I really do love you and that's why I'm doing this. I promise, I'll call you in the morning, okay?"

He nodded, though I could tell that he really didn't agree. With the way he looked at me, I knew I had to get him out of that hotel room.

"Be careful driving home." I stood and tightened the belt of my robe. "The roads are probably pretty slippery if it's snowing out there." I glanced out the window.

Chase stood. "If I don't hear from you, I'll call you in the morning."

"Don't you have to watch film with the team tomorrow?"

"Nope. Since we won, Coach gave us tomorrow off." Chase slowly slipped back into his coat.

I didn't want him to leave, but it was best. My hormones were raging and my heart was pounding.

I walked him to the door.

"Good night," he whispered; then he walked out and gently closed the door.

I waited until I could no longer hear his footsteps in the hall, then collapsed on the bed and started to weep. Only a few minutes passed before I heard another knock on the door.

"Zoe?" Chase's voice filtered in.

I sat up and wiped my tears. "What did you forget?" I said through the closed door. I looked around the room but didn't see keys or anything.

"Zoe?" he called again, not answering my question.

I opened the door and stared at him, wondering what he was up to.

"The guy at the desk told me I shouldn't leave. He said the storm was blowing in real bad. I went outside and I couldn't even see my car, the snow is falling so hard."

He walked over to the window and pulled back the curtain as if he wanted to prove it to me.

All I could see were sheets of white, on the ground and falling through the air. I sighed, relieved that Chase hadn't tried to drive in the weather. The last thing I wanted was for something bad to happen to him.

"Well, I'm glad you didn't try to go home in that. I suppose you'll have to get a room here."

"Can't," he said. "There was only one room available, and I let someone else have it."

I glared at him, wondering if he had done that just so he'd have to share my room.

"Guess I'll have to stay here," he said, taking off his coat again. As he did, he stopped and hollered, "Ouch!" His face winced in pain and he grabbed his shoulder.

Suddenly my anger was gone. "What's wrong?" I asked, rushing to his side.

"I bruised my shoulder during the game today. The

trainer looked at it and iced it down and he gave me another couple of packs so I could take care of it tonight."

"And where are the ice packs?"

"Oh, I'm having them brought up."

"What? I didn't know this hotel had valets." I glared at him with doubt in my eyes.

"It doesn't. I saw a homeless guy sitting outside the lobby. I couldn't bear the thought of him staying out all night in that blizzard. So I offered to get him a room. He insisted on bringing my gym bag up here. Guess he wanted to earn his lodging."

There was a hesitant knock on the door and Chase opened it. An old, pale, rough-looking gentleman stood there holding a small leather bag. Chase accepted it with a smile.

"Thank you again, Mr. Farr. You been a blessing, truly a blessing."

"Order whatever you want from room service, Mr. Sheely. The bill's on me."

The man paused, and nodded, as if he weren't able to say any more words. I was sure I saw tears in his eyes. "You saved me, Mr. Farr. I didn't think I was gonna make it through the night without some food and shelter. But I just kept quotin' from the Twenty-third Psalm, and God sent you my way."

"The Lord is watching out for both of us, Mr. Sheely."

"I reckon so." The man shook Chase's hand. "Well, good night."

"Good night." Chase shut the door. "Nice guy."

I felt bad, thinking that Chase had given up the last

room just so this old man could have shelter. "That was really sweet of you," I said, marveling again at what a wonderful man he was.

"I'm just trying to do my part." He took his bag to the dressing area and dropped it on the counter. "I can't save the world, but it feels good to know I might have saved one man from freezing to death."

He came back into the room and eased into the chair by the fireplace. I opened his bag and pulled out the ice packs and a tube of medicated ointment. "Here," I said, "let me get you fixed up."

Chase winced again as he slipped off his shirt. I gasped when I saw his abs up close. He was unbelievably fine.

"That feels good," he murmured as I rubbed the ointment into his shoulder.

"You feel tight on this side too," I said as I worked my hands from one shoulder to the other.

Chase moaned. I gently let my thumbs slide down his back, then worked them in circular motions.

"So, tell me," I said, wanting to get us talking about something other than what my hands were doing and what I was feeling. "How does it feel to be a big star?"

"I don't know about a big star." He chuckled. "But it does feel nice. You know how I felt when I came back to Miami?" he asked. But I didn't respond, knowing that he wanted to continue. "I was jobless, with no prospects in my future. I could have been like Mr. Sheely, but God was merciful."

"Do you ever wonder if it might all end soon? That as quickly as God showed you He could do it, He could take it away, just like that?" I pressed my fingers into his shoulders.

"I can't really worry about tomorrow," Chase said, his muscles relaxing under my touch. "Life has so many uncertainties. And tomorrow is not even promised to us. But I don't have any fear about my football career because I've really put it in God's hands. He knows what He's doing. That's totally evident. I couldn't have planned my career any better." He paused and I continued to work my finger magic.

Finally, he said, "The Lord has a calling on each of our lives, Zoe. A lot of people never realize what their calling is." Chase sat up, completely focused on what he was saying. "They go through life never living up to their full potential in Christ. If I have any kind of fear, I guess that's what it would be. I want to make sure I don't miss my calling."

His words and his faith inspired me. Material things meant nothing to him. I longed to have Chase's attitude.

He leaned back again and I continued my massage.

"God can use a great athlete to win souls for Him, and I believe that's why He put me in this position. Not for me to get rich or gain fame, but to win souls for Him. I want to make sure I do that. I haven't been witnessing enough. I've been concentrating on my skills so I don't lose the job. But I have to step back and realize God will give me what I need. Sure, I need to be prepared. But I need to be about His business first."

I stared at my hands kneading his muscles and suddenly stopped. Like an electric shock, the Holy Spirit revealed to me that my hands didn't belong on this man's body.

I walked to the window and watched the snowflakes fall from the sky as quickly as raindrops. I opened the balcony door and stepped outside. I shivered, but stayed and held out my hand, allowing snowflakes to touch my fingers. I wanted the snow to make me clean, the cold air to wash away my impure thoughts.

Most folks said it was too early in the year for snow in Seattle. However, as my eyes confirmed those weren't raindrops, I knew God worked miracles anytime. And maybe, just maybe, as the snow came early this year, God could work out a miracle for me.

Chase came up behind me and placed his coat around my shoulders. "Come back in, baby. It's cold."

"See that snow?" I said, my voice trembling because of the temperature. "I wish I could be that pure."

He hugged me from behind. "We all do. We're striving to get there."

I let him draw me back inside and to the fireplace. We sat together on the rug, staring silently into the flames as I warmed back up.

"What's *your* greatest fear?" he asked minutes later.

I hesitated, then said, "I have so many. I guess I need to trust God more."

"What's the fear on your mind right now?"

"Similar to yours, I guess. Not that I won't meet my own potential in Christ, but that I'll somehow keep other people from reaching theirs." I looked up at him, the glow of the fireplace lighting up his gorgeous face. "I don't want to hinder you."

"What makes you think you could do that?"

I leaned forward and kissed him passionately, letting our tongues touch. When I pulled away, I looked into his eyes and knew I'd given him the answer to his question. I got up, grabbed a pillow and blanket from the bed and headed to the pull-out couch. "You sleep on the bed tonight. Your shoulder needs the firmness of the mattress."

"No, that's okay," he protested.

I looked at him. "Do it for me." I tossed the blanket onto the couch and lay down, facing away from him.

But even when I heard him get into the bed and turn off the light, I didn't sleep. I tossed and turned all night. It may have been blistering cold outside, but our room was beyond hot. Not from the heater or the fire, but from the burning passion that was smoldering between us. The heated kiss we'd exchanged made my body yearn for him.

Hours later, I rolled over, and in the darkness, I peered at the bed. Chase was sleeping like a baby. I got up quietly, crept into the bathroom, brushed my teeth and hair and took off my nightgown. Then I tiptoed to the fireplace and lit the two thick oblong candles with the propane lighter that sat on the mantel. I stood back and admired the romantic atmosphere their soft glow created.

I crossed to the bed and gently peeled back the covers. Without waking Chase, I slithered in and pressed my body against his. He was just as naked as I was. I kissed his bare chest. He grabbed the back of my head and squeezed my face to his as passion took over.

Chase made me feel like I'd never felt before. He kissed me with a passion and touched me with a gentleness that I'd never felt before. For minutes, our love built and I knew we were about to become one. I panted with desire. I had never wanted anything so much in my life.

"Yes," I whispered, wanting Chase so badly.

Suddenly he pulled away.

"Don't stop," I whispered. "I know you want this as much as I do. We love each other."

He hesitated, but only for a moment before he kissed me again, even more passionately. His hands wandered over my body, and my hands were all over him, everywhere they longed to be. His awesome moves on the football field didn't compare to what he was doing to me in bed.

He caressed me like a pro, and every part of me loved it. Actually, not every part. My spirit didn't, but that part was small, easily overpowered by everything that felt wonderful. This was what I had been dreaming of, and it was better than all of my fantasies combined. It was better than I could have hoped for. I continued to lead Chase down the path we'd been avoiding, quickly approaching the point of no return.

We were in dangerous territory. We had ignored all the warning signs and stepped into the storm anyway. I opened my eyes and glanced outside. The storm was still raging, and I wondered if we would be saved from our own personal blizzard.

Chapter 9

It was as if Chase heard my thoughts and he pushed me away.

"Zoe, we have to stop. Please, girl, stop." Chase moaned as he tried to push me away.

I heard him, but my mind blocked him out. I couldn't quit and held him as if I didn't know how to let go. I didn't believe he really wanted to stop. I was pleasing him and he was doing the same for me. There was no way he was going to make me stop.

All of a sudden, Chase flung me away. I landed on the floor, thumping on my backside.

"Girl, didn't I tell you to stop!"

I blinked for a moment, then crawled back onto the bed, but as soon as I got in, he jumped out. He reached for his shorts from the floor beside the bed and pulled them on.

"What's wrong?" I whined. "Wasn't I making you feel good?"

"Girl, this ain't about feelin' good. This is about honoring God. And if you ain't about that, then we clearly can't be in the same room together." He grabbed his jeans and sweatshirt off the back of the chair and frantically began dressing.

The thought of him leaving in such anger frightened me. I didn't want to lose him. I couldn't.

A repetitive banging on the window infiltrated my thoughts. I watched as Chase, fully dressed, went to the window and pulled the curtain back. "Look, I'm sorry," he said. "This is my fault too. I shouldn't have slept in this room, dangling temptation in front of us." Chunks of hail the size of golf balls were falling onto the balcony.

Chase turned away from the window, letting the curtain fall back. "I'm going down to the lobby. Maybe somebody canceled or didn't show up and I can get a room."

I glanced at the clock on the bed table. "Chase, it's three-thirty in the morning."

"There's always somebody at the front desk." He grabbed his coat and the leather bag with his ice packs and ointment. Just before he reached the door, I jumped from the bed and touched his arm. He stopped but did not turn around.

"Are you angry?" I asked.

"No," he assured me softly. He opened the door. "I just have to get out of here. I'll call you later."

When the door closed, I stared at it for several minutes. Realization slowly hit me. My man had walked out on me.

At that moment, I thought about a girl I knew in high school who'd been date raped. I'd been furious when she told me the guy didn't stop when she asked him to, told him to, begged him to. She swallowed her embarrassment and took the jerk to court.

But the guy argued, "She led me on. I knew she wanted me to make her feel good, so that's what I did."

It dawned on me that I had done the same thing now with Chase. I dropped to my knees and sobbed uncontrollably.

It looked like Fawn had been right. What if my actions had damaged Chase's walk with the Lord or poisoned him against me? I had probably caused irreparable harm.

At least thirty minutes passed before I got off my knees. I listened to the hail pelting the balcony, and for a brief moment, I pathetically wished I was out there, with ice balls pounding my pitiful body.

I stared at the candles on the fireplace mantel. They had burned so long the wick was gone. The light was completely extinguished. The symbolism frightened me and made me shudder. What if I had done the same thing to my relationship with Chase?

I looked at the bed but knew I wouldn't be able to get back into the place where I had lain with Chase. So, I returned to the pull-out.

"Lord," I cried out loud. "Why do I feel this way? Why do I want him so badly? Couldn't You just take these feelings away from me? Lord, please don't let this be the end for me and Chase. Oh, Lord, I'm so sorry!"

Part of me knew where the deep sexual desire came from. I could still see me at eleven. I was starting to develop and my mama didn't really like it. "Mr. Jenkins is coming over, girl," she said. "Go put on something. I plan to give him love; I don't want him lusting for you. Shoot, one day when you get grown, you'll understand how to keep a man. Now, gon'. Shoot, we got to eat. Gon'."

Though my heart still ached, I found some comfort in

talking to God. I prayed that He had heard me, and I hoped that a new day would straighten things out. Finally, I drifted off to sleep.

When I opened my eyes just a few hours later, the first thing I saw was the empty bed. The recollection of the previous night's disaster hit me full force.

I checked the clock on the nightstand. Eight A.M. Chase had left almost five hours before. I got up, threw on the clothes I'd worn yesterday and looked out the balcony window. A thick carpet of snow covered the ground, but no new flurries or hailstones filled the air.

I picked up the phone and called the front desk. "Please put me through to Chase Farr's room."

"Sorry, ma'am," the clerk said coolly. "We don't have a Chase Farr listed."

"Come on. I know he's in this hotel."

"I'm sorry, ma'am."

I sighed. Either the hotel was trying to protect a famous professional athlete from aggressive female fans, or Chase had already checked out.

Finally, I slammed the phone down and then frantically dialed the apartment. When our answering machine came on, I punched in the code to check messages.

"You have two messages," the machine informed me. The first was from my mother. I hadn't talked to her since the week after I moved to Seattle, when I called to let her know where I was and that I was okay.

"I need to talk to you, Zoe," my mother's recorded voice said. "It's serious, so please call as soon as you can."

I did need to call my mother, but I didn't believe there was any real emergency. She was probably being overly dramatic just to get me to call. Besides, talking to her wasn't really important to me at this moment. My priority was to find Chase and try to straighten things out.

I pressed the button and desperately hoped that the second call on the machine was from Chase. I almost dropped the phone when an unfamiliar female voice started speaking.

"Hi, Chase. It's Waverly Phillips. Thanks for dropping me off last night. I don't know what I would have done without you. You truly were my hero. Hey, it was fun cheering for you at the game. Keep up the great work. See you soon."

"What?" I screamed, slamming down the receiver. I racked my brain trying to remember all of the Storm cheerleaders' names. I was pretty sure Waverly Phillips was one of them.

But cheerleaders didn't go to away games with the team. Who was this chick? Where was Chase? What was going on?

I paced the floor. I needed help. Maybe I should call my mom. But she wouldn't be any help with this. I could never tell her what was going on between me and Chase. She had judged me all my life. I had never been able to measure up to her standards. She was the last person I could count on to give me the help I needed now.

During my childhood, Mom had always been too involved in her life to talk to me, much less offer motherly advice. I had basically raised myself. I loved my mom, and I respected her because she did what she had to do to feed me and my brother. But I knew I wanted a different life for myself.

Still, I wanted to hear her voice. I dialed her number. "Hey, Mom."

"Zoe, girl, it's about time you called me back. Honey, I really have to see you."

"Mom, my life is pretty crazy right now," I said, almost wishing that I hadn't made the call.

"Well, I need you to get home as soon as you can."

"What about what I need, Mom? Can't we talk about that for once?"

For a moment, nothing but silence crossed the telephone wire. "Okay, baby. Tell me what's on your mind."

Now that she'd offered, I didn't know where to start.

"I saw that your friend is doing real well at football," she said, giving me an opening.

My friend. "Yeah, Mom. Chase is doin' great." I couldn't say anything else around the lump in my throat.

"You haven't called, so I assumed y'all were doin' real good." Another pause. "You're being a lady up there, right?"

Bitter words that had been building for years leaped from my throat. I remembered all of those times, after my dad died, when my mother had one guy after another in the house. But no one ever stayed longer than one night. "I learned how to be a lady from you, Mom, so what do you think I'm doing?"

"Zoe!"

I immediately regretted my comment, but I didn't feel the need to take it back. "You know what? This was a bad idea. I knew you wouldn't understand. I'll call you later. I gotta go."

"But, Zoe, I need to talk to you."

I heard a knock on the door. "I'll call you back, Mom." I dropped the receiver onto its base and raced to the door. There stood Chase, looking amazing.

I threw my arms around him. "I'm so sorry, baby. I didn't mean to push." I wasn't sure what I could say to make it better. I pulled back and looked into his eyes. They held a depth of despair that frightened me. "What is it? What's wrong?"

He came into the room and sat in a chair beside the window. He looked up at me, dejection in his eyes. "I love you, Zoe. But there's no way this can work if we don't put God first. We can't build a relationship on sex. I don't want to lose you, but if that's what it comes down to . . ."

I sat in the chair next to him. "Chase, I am so sorry for what happened last night. It's just that I have wanted you for so long."

"I understand. I feel the same way. But my relationship with God is the most important thing to me. I want a wife who walks with God, and, Zoe, I don't know if you do." He reached for my hand. "Can you understand that?"

I looked down at his fingers entwined in mine. I ached to do more than just hold hands. But I was just happy that he had come back and we were together. I nodded my agreement. "I understand, Chase."

He smiled. "I hope we can make this work, Zoe." He kissed me lightly on the cheek. "I do love you, girl."

The blizzard and hail storm cleared up, and so did my relationship with Chase. I checked out of the hotel and moved back into the apartment, both of us agreeing that we would end the arrangement if either one of us couldn't keep our hormones in check.

Most of the games left in the season were away games, and between that and practices and interviews and public appearances, Chase would be gone quite a bit. And I was busy with my job, so I figured that we could handle it—at least I would try my best.

In addition, Chase got me to agree to something that he was sure would help us.

"We should start going to Bible study."

"But what about the couples group that we've been going to."

"That's been good, the few times we've gone. But I think we need a bit more help, don't you?"

I agreed. We hadn't found a church home in Seattle yet, and we needed some sort of spiritual counseling.

On Friday morning, I went with Fawn and Shay to a women's group led by the Storm's chaplain's wife, Amy Wilcox. She asked each of us to talk about how our relationships were going. Fawn openly discussed her marriage, and Shay talked about her engagement. But they'd both known Amy for a while. I felt uncomfortable talking to a stranger about my private life. Especially after the way Fawn had lectured me.

So, I kept my mouth shut—for the most part. I was relieved when Shay announced that she was starting to struggle in the area of sexual purity.

"I just don't know if I can do it. I love Byron so much it just seems natural to go there. Especially since we've finally set the wedding day for Christmas and it's coming soon. But sometimes, it seems like three months is the same as forever. And truthfully, Byron's not helping any. What am I supposed to do?"

"Well, at least you guys live in separate places,"

Fawn interjected. "Zoe, I still don't understand how you can stay in that apartment, facing temptation day and night."

I didn't know how the attention had shifted so quickly to me. "It's not like we share a bed," I said, crossing my arms. "We don't even share a bedroom."

"But either of you could sneak into the other one's room easily enough. Besides, it's not just about sex. If you and Chase live together now, what happens if you get married? What will you have to look forward to?"

"I have a lot to look forward to," I blurted out, knowing I sounded defensive.

"Like what?"

Her comment had caught me so off guard that I couldn't think of any examples at the moment, so I pressed my lips together and remained silent.

Fawn smiled triumphantly. She continued as if her opinion were the only one that counted. "It's a special thing to know that when you walk down that aisle, you are finally going to know everything about the man who has chosen you to go through life with him. But if you've already seen him when he wakes up, brushes his teeth, and all that, you shortchange yourself."

Shay giggled. "I'm not sure that watching Byron brush his teeth is all that great a thing to look forward to."

Fawn glared at her.

Amy cleared her throat. "The most important point in what Fawn is saying is that by living together, even if you're not sexually active, you blow your witness to anyone who is trying to see Christ through you. God's Word says we are to flee every appearance of evil." She turned to me. "I'd hate to see you or your witness ruined, Zoe."

Her words sounded the same as Fawn's. However, she spoke with compassion and concern, and that left me with no argument.

"The male-female relationship is a difficult one," Amy continued. "Life is so up and down. If your relationship is not based solidly on Christ, anything can come in its way. A wrong play, a bad day, a lost game. The smallest thing will upset the balance."

Chase and I got along great, but I remembered a few shaky times when he came home from a game where he hadn't done his best. And when I really thought about it, I'd probably fallen into bad moods after a hard day on the job too. But who didn't?

Amy picked up a light blue paperback. "I'd like to go through a study with you ladies based on this book," she said. "In order to be a good wife, fiancée or girlfriend, you've got to be confident with who you are in Christ. You can really contribute something special to your relationship if it's founded on Christian principles."

She handed us copies of the book. I thumbed through mine. It looked complicated. And boring.

"Focus on building a close relationship with God," Amy continued, "before you try to have a good relationship with your significant other. Then, when the trials come, when unexpected things arise, when the sea gets rough and stormy, you'll have an anchor. And you can *be* an anchor, to encourage your mate when he's down or weak."

The book seemed a chore, but I was intrigued by Amy's words. I wanted to understand what she was saying.

Amy turned to Shay. "Honey, God can help you resist the temptations to be with Byron until the time comes. There are a lot of other things that are more important in a relationship than physical intimacy, things that will keep you together. You need to build on those things now. In a marriage, the physical part should be the icing on the cake, not the only thing you eat. If you just eat dessert, that's not healthy."

We sat in silence, absorbing Amy's words, staring at the blue books, lost in our own thoughts.

"Speaking of dessert," Amy said, giving us a break from what was going on in our minds, "Fawn brought something that looks absolutely heavenly."

It was what we needed. We scurried to the buffet table, where we chatted about calories and diets and other insignificant subjects. Even as we ate the finger sandwiches and vegetable quiche, we kept away from what we'd been discussing. I was relieved. I didn't want to be the center of attention. Especially not this kind of attention.

I was the first one to prepare to leave and Amy walked me to the door.

"I'm praying for you, Zoe," she said simply.

There was so much in her words. I knew she didn't agree with my living arrangements, but I didn't hear any judgment in her voice.

"Thank you," I said, and squeezed her hand.

"I hope you'll come back."

I nodded but didn't commit. I wasn't sure if I wanted to put myself in this situation again.

As I drove home, though, I realized I was really looking forward to the next session with Amy. I sincerely desired to do what God wanted me to do in my relationship with Chase. But I knew I wasn't winning the battle. Maybe just listening and talking with Amy would help me get to where I truly wanted to go.

I sat in the living room, watching Chase run up and down the football field on the TV screen. As usual, he was awesome.

Chase truly was the Storm. He carried the team from a motivational standpoint, and his offense made the defense rise. The other offensive players scored more as well—no one wanted to be outshone that much. Every time Chase played, it was obvious that God had anointed him.

When the final whistle blew, one of the network announcers ran onto the field, pulling Chase to the side.

"Well, Chase, here we are again," the announcer said. "Once again, you've been named 'player of the game.' Congratulations on having another top-notch game."

"Thank you, but as always, I give all honor and glory to God."

I shook my head as I watched. It was amazing—the platform that professional sports had afforded him. Here he was, on network television, with millions of people watching him, announcing that his talent came from the Lord. God was blessing him.

As he continued to talk, nodding and waving his hands in the air as he spoke, I started feeling a heavy dose of desire. I longed for him to be home. He wouldn't arrive until much later that evening, but the thought of being with him would keep me awake well into the night.

I wanted to give him something special to congratulate

him for making MVP. After his first victory, I'd bought him a tie. This time, I thought he deserved something much more special. I imagined myself sitting in the living room chair, wearing the tie I had bought him. And nothing else. *Am I bad to think these thoughts? Isn't it natural to want him?* I kept asking myself.

For the rest of the evening, I tried to think of what I could do for Chase. Something special. After all, we'd been together for a while now. Maybe it was time to take our relationship to the next level. I thought about what Fawn and Amy had said, but they didn't understand. They were married. It was different being single in today's times.

Later that night, I heard a racket outside. Peering out the window, I saw it was hailing. It looked like another blizzard was on the way. I prayed that it would not delay Chase's arrival home. I had already made up my mind. I knew what I was going to do for him.

It was after one o'clock in the morning when Chase walked through the door. I sat in the living room, but I had all the lights turned off.

As he reached for the switch, I said, "Leave the lights off."

I could see him trying to peer through the dark, trying to find me. I walked right up to him and took his suitcase from his hand.

"You played an awesome game today," I whispered. "I missed you." I dropped his bag onto the floor, then grabbed Chase's cold hands and placed them firmly on my warm breasts.

It didn't take longer than a moment for Chase to shove me away and flip on the lights. He stared at my naked body, then pushed me aside.

"You know, all through the return flight," he ranted as he stomped down the hall, "I couldn't wait to get home so I could tell you about my game and tell you how much I missed you. But all you've been thinking about is sex. We talked about this, Zoe!"

He returned to the living room with a bath towel and tossed it to me. I wrapped it around my trembling body.

"Zoe, you're gonna have to get out of here. If you don't, you're just gonna make me mess up. You've got to leave, tonight."

"Chase, please, let me explain." I started to cry. "I just wanted—"

"No. I'm tired of hearing the excuses. We've been through this over and over again. You know where I stand, and I thought you were standing with me. Are you trying to make me fall?"

I stood, shivering in the towel, staring at this angry, beautiful man. "Chase, I—"

"If you won't go, then I will." He picked up his bag and walked out the door without another word.

I stared at the open door. Tears streamed down my cheeks. I had made a big mistake, and I didn't think there would ever be a way to resolve this. The blow of our relationship's being over hit as hard as the outside hail.

Chapter 10

"It'll be okay, Zoe," Shay said, stroking my arm in an effort to comfort me. "Please don't cry like this."

"You don't understand," I declared, sobbing into my pillow. "It's not okay. It's over. I kept pushing and pushing. Now I've pushed Chase away completely."

"But do you have to go back to Miami?" she asked, looking at the suitcases that I had pulled from the closet. "Don't you think you should talk to Chase about this first?"

I sat up on the bed. "He hasn't called me all week. He doesn't want to talk to me."

"But it's only been a week. Maybe he just needs more time."

I shook my head. "I know Chase. It's over." I sighed. "I came to Seattle to get away from my depressing life in Miami, and now I'm more depressed than ever."

"Maybe you should stop running," Shay suggested softly. "If you go back to Miami with things the way they are between you and Chase, you'll just be running away again."

"Or maybe I need to stand up for myself and get my own life," I said, trying to be strong. "If I have to depend on anyone, it should be my family." I looked at the telephone. "My mom has been calling and leaving messages, but I've been ignoring them. I need to go home and find out what's up with her. Who knows? Maybe we can finally straighten things out between us."

I pushed myself from the bed and walked to the closet. For the first time, I began giving serious thought to why my mom had been calling and leaving such insistent messages. She'd never bugged me this much.

As thoughts wandered through my mind, I began to worry about my family. Hopefully, my brother hadn't gotten into any trouble. I shook my head. No, Alonzo was probably fine or he would have called me. Most likely, Mom just couldn't handle me being all the way across the country, so far from her reach.

I turned back to Shay. "So, how's Chase doing?" I asked as casually as I could, though I knew I wasn't fooling Shay.

"He's fine," Shay said. "Well, not really fine. After practice every day, he goes straight to Byron's place; then he just eats, watches football videos and goes to sleep."

"It's good that he can forget about me and fall asleep so easily," I said bitterly, yanking blouses off the hangers in my closet. I hadn't been able to eat or sleep all week.

"Zoe, don't talk like that. You've got to snap out of this. It isn't good for a person to be down for so long."

"What's the big deal?" I pulled open the top dresser drawer and scooped up all of my underwear, tossing it into the bag. "Why shouldn't I stay depressed for as long as I feel like it?"

Shay sat on my bed, watching me with sad eyes. "Well, if nothing else, it's bound to affect your job. Look at you.

Thinking about going back to Miami, when you have such a wonderful position here."

I stopped moving and glared at her. "Oh, didn't I tell you? Blanche called yesterday. She doesn't need me anymore. She said that the jobs that are coming up are small, so she doesn't require an assistant and couldn't afford one anyway."

"Surely that's just temporary," Shay said.

I resumed my packing, clearing out all the drawers in the dresser. "She has something coming up in a few months, but it's not a guarantee."

"How can she do that to you?" Shay asked.

I chuckled, though I wasn't happy. "Blanche said that I would be fine because my boyfriend is Chase Farr!"

"She doesn't know you guys broke up, huh?"

"I didn't see the need to blab it to the whole world," I said, trying to zip the suitcase.

"Well, I'm glad you told me," Shay said. "I really do care about you."

I looked into Shay's brown eyes. "I know," I said softly. "Thanks." Then, not wanting to get distracted by any more sad emotions, I grabbed the second suitcase and started walking through the apartment, grabbing incidentals that belonged to me.

Shay followed me. "Zoe, I don't want you to move away. What about my engagement party? You promised to help me."

"Sorry," I mumbled, stopping at the table and lifting a picture frame. I held up the five-by-seven photo frame with the image of Chase and me at the park. This was taken when we first arrived in Seattle.

"I have an idea," Shay said as I stared at the photo. "I know you were going to volunteer your services, but Byron would pay you to put our party together. Then you wouldn't have to go . . . at least not right away."

I shook my head and placed the picture back on the table. "Thanks, Shay, but no thanks. Putting one party together, even if I charged Byron full price, wouldn't be enough to cover two months' rent on an apartment of my own."

"Oh, come on," Shay protested. "At least that would be a start, and who knows what would happen with Blanche by then. We had a party for family a while ago. He just wants another for his friends. Something to do. Help me!"

Over Shay's continued pleas, I walked through the apartment for the final time, making sure I wouldn't be leaving anything behind. I didn't want to have to come back here for anything.

Finally, I turned to Shay and there were tears in our eyes. "I'm sorry, girl, but it really is over for me."

Shay nodded, accepting, but not agreeing with my words. "Listen, I want to say this to you because I've grown to love ya. I know you want Chase, but, girl—want God. If you want a lova' . . . What do you think has kept me? Try Him."

I couldn't be mad. But I surely didn't want to hear it. However, I put aside my initial hesitance and took in what my friend said. Could the philosophy that worked for her work for me? Who knew.

Not pushing, Shay changed subjects and asked, "Do you still want me to take you to the airport?"

This time, I nodded, because I knew that if I said anything, my tears would flow.

I turned back to the bedroom to get my suitcases. It was time to leave.

I closed my eyes tightly as the airplane jerked again, flying through the turbulence. It had been a rocky trip. I opened one eye slightly and peeked through the plane's window. The lightning outside frightened me. I wondered if we should be flying in such a mad storm.

Lord, I prayed silently as I gripped the side of the seat, *I don't like being on this plane right now. But then, I know You don't like what I've been doing with my life lately. I realize that I deserve all the rotten things that have happened to me. I've been so selfish. All I had to do was stop being so pigheaded and listen to what Fawn was telling me. But I ignored her, and I ended up pushing Chase away. I couldn't see it then, but I see it now. Unfortunately, it's too late.*

The plane dipped again. I pulled my seat belt tighter. *Maybe this is it for me,* I thought as I squeezed my eyelids together again. *Maybe this is how my life is supposed to end. When I finally realize my mistakes, I die in a plane crash.*

I shook my head, thinking how sad that would be. What would be worse was that Chase probably wouldn't even miss me. I forced myself to stop thinking such morbid thoughts.

Lord, I said inside, continuing my prayer, *my heart is so heavy right now. I'm going home, but to what? I know something is up with my mother. And I don't know what's going on with Devyn or Aisha. I don't know if they've gotten over their drama.* I just didn't know what to expect from this trip back across the country.

Tears streamed down my face, though I wasn't sure if they were from my thoughts or from the way the plane continued to dip.

When the plane dropped and rocked again, I grabbed the hand of the young woman next to me as if she were my best friend. She started reciting the Lord's Prayer and I joined in with her.

Boom!

We both jumped, our eyes wide at the loud sound.

"That was the engine!" one of the passengers near the front of the plane screamed. The violent shaking of the plane increased, tossing cups and peanut wrappers everywhere.

I was certain I was going to die. This was the end and it made me look back over my life. I had let the Lord down in so many ways. I needed to repent.

I had so much to repent for. I remembered when I was twelve, when my mom's older brother, Sammy, showed me centerfold pictures in a girlie magazine and then asked me to pose for him. Though I never did it, I often thought about it. I posed alone several times in front of my bedroom mirror, imagining what it would be like to be one of those gorgeous models.

I remembered losing my virginity at fourteen to one of my brother's friends, who was a senior in high school. Not wanting him to think I was a kid, I did it willingly, easily, even though I hated every minute.

Then I thought about my times at college, and about when I fell head over heels for Devyn. We were intimate at least four times a week, and I was always running to the doctor for a pregnancy test.

After graduating from college, I should have been smarter. But I still messed up a wonderful relationship with Chase because I couldn't control my desire for sex.

Looking back, I knew why my life was so messed up. I had never really given everything to Christ. I'd become a Christian years ago, and I knew I had grace. But I never exercised that grace for myself. I didn't do what God does, and forget my sins. I kept carrying my past transgressions with me. It was no wonder that I always felt so burdened.

I didn't want to spend the last moments of my life focusing on my pain. I wanted to spend the time letting God know that I was sorry for my sins. Not a few, but all of them. I desperately wanted to become a person after God's own heart, even if only for a few seconds.

The oxygen masks sprang down from above. Following the attendant's instructions, we placed our masks over our noses. I was shaking uncontrollably. I tried to breathe deeply, to calm my trembling.

The aircraft tilted dramatically to the left, and one of the doors on the overhead bin flew open.

I screamed.

Several bags came sliding out, one punching a man in the eye. A flight attendant wobbled down the aisle to see if the passenger was all right.

Screams now filled the cabin.

The intercom came to life as a stewardess at the front clicked it on.

"The captain has just informed us that we are going to make an emergency landing. We need to have everyone brace in the crash position."

I followed the instructions as she asked us to lean forward and place our heads between our knees. It was hard to do between my tears and trembling.

But I held my ankles, as instructed. All concern I had for my past was dissolved. I had given everything to God and was looking forward to what I imagined heaven to be. I was ready to release my life to Him. So I prayed for peace, for myself and for those around me, especially the pilots.

"Lord," the blond girl next to me named LeAnn Terry cried, "what did I do to deserve this?"

I peeked over at her. "It's okay," I assured her. "I don't think you, or anyone else here, did anything bad. You know, maybe God just needs us to go home."

"But I'm not ready," LeAnn screamed.

I closed my eyes. "Lord, help this girl," I prayed over the screams and cries that filled the cabin. "I don't know what she's going through. But help her find her peace. Lord, give us all peace."

As the plane made its descent, I squeezed my eyes tighter.

"I'm ready, Lord," I whispered.

A moment later, the plane touched the ground. Even though I was supposed to stay down, I lifted my head and peeked through the window. I could almost see the wind, whipping around the airplane as the pilot glided us to a complete halt.

We stopped, and for several moments, only silence filled our space.

Then the girl cried out, "Thank you, Lord. Thank you!"

Everyone in the plane cheered and clapped.

"Well, folks," the captain said over the intercom. "We are in Dallas. I know this isn't where you expected to be, but we wanted to get us all somewhere safely."

We stood and rushed toward the emergency exit doors, where the flight attendants and several Good Samaritan passengers helped us down the inflatable emergency slides. When I was settled safely onto the tarmac, I wanted to get on my knees, kiss the ground and thank God. But I stood next to the girl who had been sitting next to me and surveyed the damaged plane. Smoke and fire billowed from one of the engines, making it difficult to see much of anything in the dark.

"I cannot believe we got out of there," the girl cried.

I put my arms around her. "I know. We're blessed."

Many of the passengers were crying—men and women alike. But I didn't have any tears. I guess I was cried out.

I helped my new friend into one of the emergency vehicles that was taking passengers to the terminals.

"Thank you," she said to me.

"For what?"

"For reminding me through all of this that God was with us. I wouldn't have made it without you," she said. "You are definitely one of God's angels."

I smiled. No one had ever said anything like that to me before. And if she only knew why I was even on that plane, she would have known that being called one of God's angels was the biggest compliment anyone could have ever given me.

When she asked me for my address, I frowned.

But she reassured me quickly. "I just want to find a way to say thank you for all that you did for me tonight."

I shrugged and gave her my mother's address. I didn't really expect to ever hear from her again. She was probably just being polite.

When she stopped chatting, I was finally able to lean back in the minivan and close my eyes.

Dear Lord, I silently began my prayer. *I want to always remember these moments. I want to always remember what it felt like to think I had reached the end of my earthly journey. From this point, I want to live my life only pleasing You. I know that it was only because of You that the plane landed safely. I could feel Your guiding hand. If You could do that, Father, You can surely do the same thing with my life.* I paused and opened my eyes. This was certainly going to be the first day of the rest of my life.

The next day, as I drove into my mother's neighborhood, I remembered how much I hated the projects. I detested the roaches, loud music, winos, random gun shootings and everything else associated with living there. But after the horrific plane ride, I was just excited to be home.

And I was glad to be home so that I could resolve old issues with my mother. We had a lot of talking to do. I felt that I'd been damaged so much as a child, and the only way to get rid of all I was carrying was to get it out in the open. After we cleared the air, I hoped my mother and I could have the kind of mother-daughter relationship I knew we both wanted and needed.

I barely stopped my rented car in front of my mother's building before she came running outside. She gripped me tightly when I got out of the car.

"I've been so worried ever since you called from Dallas," she said, trying to control her sobbing.

"I'm okay, Mom," I assured her.

"I don't know how you were able to get on another plane after that," she said, pulling back to take a good look at me.

"It was scary," I admitted, "but I knew God had everything under control. If the plane went down, then that was what He wanted with my life."

She peered at me, obviously surprised at my confident words. I opened my trunk and pulled out my suitcases. Last night, as I was settling in at the hotel, the airline called and told me that my luggage was saved. Although it didn't matter to me at that point, I was grateful. I gave one suitcase to my mother and then I carried the other.

My mother couldn't take her eyes or her hands off me. I was a bit surprised. My mother had never been very affectionate, but I could tell from her outpouring of emotion that she loved me far more than I had ever given her credit for. I longed to tell her how much I cared about her and appreciated her. But she didn't give me the chance. As soon as we were inside her two-bedroom apartment and we sat down on the sofa, she began talking.

"I'm sorry I wasn't the best mother to you and Alonzo," she said, her voice catching in her throat. "I've done things in my life that I'm not proud of. But I sure am proud of you. You are such a blessing." She patted my knee, tears misting her eyes. "I've been praying for you to come home for so long."

I was surprised again—this time by her words. For the last several hours, I'd wondered how I was going to bring up the subject, but now my mother was saying the things I wanted to hear. I knew it was God at work. He'd given me this second chance with my life and He was giving me the opportunity to fix the things that needed fixing.

"I know, Mom. I'm sorry too," I said.

She shook her head. "You don't have anything to be sorry about. I'm just so grateful that God answered my prayers. He brought you home to see me." She pulled a tissue from the box on an end table and dabbed at her eyes. "And just in time too."

It took me a moment to understand her words. "What do you mean, Mom?" I asked, catching the seriousness in her tone. "What's wrong?" My heart began to pound.

"Sweetie," she whispered, "they found a lump." She placed her right hand over her left breast.

The look in my mother's eyes was the same one I'd seen on the blond girl's face when our plane was descending so rapidly. Her words struck me like an explosion.

Chapter 11

"Oh, Mom." I hugged her tightly. I had never embraced my mom like that before. But then, I had never thought about losing her. At that moment, I realized that my mother meant more to me than I'd ever admitted. The last thing I wanted to do was let go of her.

After several minutes, she pulled away and walked to the kitchen. Soft tears streamed down her face as she poured water into a teakettle and placed it on the stove. She pulled a package of tea bags from the cupboard and then turned to me.

"I've been battling breast cancer for years, Zoe."

"Oh my God, Mom. Why didn't you tell me?"

She shook her head. "I didn't want you to worry. No one knew, not even your brother." She paused as if she needed the time to gather strength. "Sometimes the pain is excruciating, almost more than I can bear."

I shook my head. I couldn't believe her words. I tried to think back on the time I spent with my mother, especially as I was planning my wedding. But no matter what, I couldn't remember any clues. I never saw her pain. I just never knew.

I guess I had been so wrapped up with my own life that I never gave much thought to what was going on with anyone else—especially my mother. My heart ached as I thought of all of those phone calls my mother had made to me in Seattle, and how I just ignored her. When she needed me most, I wasn't there. I was on the other side of the country, doing my own thing.

"Last year, when they detected cancer cells in my right breast, the doctors removed them. But after the surgery, I felt even worse."

It hurt to think that my mom had been going through struggles that I knew nothing about. She had actually been in the hospital and I knew nothing about it. I tried to imagine which month it was—though it could have been anytime. I didn't speak to my mother or visit her very often.

"Mom, I'm sorry I haven't been here for you." I felt like my words were lame. Though I meant them sincerely, the words sounded hollow. There was nothing I could say to erase the fact that I was not there when my mother needed me.

"I ain't gonna lie to you, Zoe. It's been rough. But God has been with me every step of the way. When I was hooked up to all those machines, He showed me that He could take me anytime He wanted. But He didn't. He wants my healing. But He's teaching me a lot through this."

My heart broke as I pictured my mother lying alone in a hospital bed, surrounded by cold machines and medical personnel who were paid to take care of her, along with dozens of other patients. No family. No cards. No flowers. And yet, she didn't seem bitter.

"I don't want you to feel bad, Zoe. I was glad that I told no one. It made me depend on God. All my life I tried to handle things myself. I did everything I could to provide for my children, trying all kinds of desperate things: drugs, men, alcohol. But if I would have just trusted God to provide for us, things could have been so much better."

The teakettle whistled, and Mom poured the hot water over the tea bags inside two chipped mugs. As we sat at the kitchen table, sipping our hot drinks, my mother explained some of the procedures she'd endured.

I listened, feeling as sorry for her as I felt for myself. "Mom, where do you stand now? What's going on with the cancer?" It was hard to even ask those questions.

"Well, you're home just in time. Tomorrow I go to the doctor to see if the chemo has worked."

"I'd like to go with you," I said, squeezing her hand.

My mother smiled for the first time. "Thanks, baby. I'd like that."

When my mother hugged me, there was more love in her little run-down two-bedroom apartment than I'd ever seen or felt in even the grandest homes I'd visited. And that made me wonder why I'd always done whatever I could to get far away from here. Because right now, there was nowhere that I wanted to be more than at home.

I stayed with my mom for a week. Helping her was a sad joy. I was overjoyed to finally be there for her. But I felt miserable that she had to go through this terrible illness.

We did get some comforting news from the doctor. It wasn't the news we wanted to hear. The cancer hadn't all disappeared, but the chemo was working. The cancer cells were being reduced.

The treatments made Mom nauseated. But she was a trouper. Knowing that it was working spurred her on to endure the pain and discomfort. And I think it helped that I was with her. I was a visual reminder that she had much to live for.

Her tenacity inspired me, and gradually, I began to see some improvement. My mother was getting better. Although she needed to take an afternoon nap every day, and she was a bit thinner, she acted like her usual healthy self in every other way.

On the third day that I spent with my mother, I picked up her mail and noticed a small package addressed to me, from an unfamiliar address. I ripped off the brown paper wrapping and found a book by Max Lucado entitled *In the Eye of the Storm*. On the first blank page was a note: "Zoe, my life is forever different because you showed me, in the eye of my storm, how to stay focused on Jesus. With Him, I got through the storm. Thanks." It was from LeAnn, the girl who sat next to me on the flight.

I sat on the couch, turned the page and started reading. The words of the book came alive. They described so well the chaos that filled my life over the last few months.

As I read the book, memories of my time with Chase came flooding back, memories that I had successfully tucked away and ignored amid all the activity surrounding my mother's illness. But now, as I thought about my life, I started feeling depressed again. I needed to keep focused so I wouldn't sink back into my sorrows. I wanted to keep my eyes on the big picture—keeping God in the center of my life. As long as I remembered that, I wouldn't be able to focus on the temptations around me. Then, before I knew it, I would be through the storm.

I read the book for almost an hour, then went into the extra bedroom and prayed before I read my Bible.

I was in the middle of John, the fourteenth chapter, when the telephone rang. My mother was still napping, so I rushed into the living room and answered, not wanting the ringing to wake her.

"Hello?" I said quietly.

"May I speak with Zoe Clarke, please?" an unfamiliar voice asked.

"Speaking," I said hesitantly.

"I'm Mr. Douglas Ware, the public-relations director for the Seattle Storm. I received your résumé a few weeks ago and I was quite impressed. So glad your Miami information is still current. I didn't have anything available at that time, but a position has just opened and I'd like to offer you the special-events coordinator."

I recalled leaving my résumé in the front office of the Seattle Storm a while back. I was told by one of the secretaries that positions probably wouldn't be open till after the season. But she said she would process my résumé anyway. Since my chances weren't good, I hadn't given a thought to it since.

"If you're interested, you could start right away," he continued, sounding a bit desperate.

"I don't understand," I said. "Are you saying I wouldn't have to interview?"

"Well, we lost the person who held the position quite suddenly," he explained. "Terrible timing, since we've had several requests for our football players to speak at various events, now that the team is doing so well. We also have a Christmas party coming up, and with our record, we wanted to do something special."

I couldn't believe what I was hearing. This job would be an incredible blessing. Just being offered the position proved that with God all things were possible, even when secretaries said otherwise! But I wondered, *Why me? Surely I wasn't the first choice.*

"We checked your references," he said as if he could hear my thoughts. "I spoke at length with your former boss, Blanche Wright, who has occasionally organized events for us. She told me that you were primarily responsible for the governor's ball and the library dedication. Those were first class. We'd really be honored if you could come on board with us."

I was excited, but then I remembered where I was. "Mr. Ware, I'm in Florida right now on a family emergency. My mother is very sick."

"Oh, I'm sorry to hear that."

"Well, actually, I think she's doing better. But before I make any decisions like this, I'd like to discuss it with her."

"I understand. But, Zoe, I hope to hear from you soon. We won't be able to hold this position open for long." As an added incentive, he gave me more details of the position: the salary, which would be more than I'd ever earned, the benefits and the vacation package. Even though I tried to contain it, my enthusiasm ballooned. I knew God was watching out for me. I wasn't even looking for a job, though it was a no-brainer that I needed one. But I had focused on staying connected with Christ, and He had provided.

I took a deep breath. The only problem was that Seattle was the last place I wanted to be. If I took this job, I would have to see Chase again. I wondered how that would feel. Of greater concern to me, though, was the thought of leaving my mother now, when she really needed me.

I paced in the living room until she rose from her nap. As I prepared sandwiches for us to nibble on, I calmly told her about the phone call from the Seattle Storm.

"So, when do you start?" she asked, her enthusiasm matching mine.

I was touched by her exuberance but needed to be sure that she wasn't acting. I had to know that she was really going to be all right without me.

"I haven't accepted the job yet, Mom," I said.

"Well, for heaven's sake, why not? It sounds perfect."

"I wanted to discuss it with you first. If you need me to stay—"

"I'll be fine," my mother assured me. "You heard the doctor. Those latest reports showed that things aren't as bad as they could be. And I've been feeling so much better this week. I honestly believe I'll keep getting better."

"Are you sure?"

"Zoe, I've never been more sure of anything in my life." She paused. "I really want you to take this position. It's the kind of work that you've been looking for."

I rushed to the table and hugged her, not wanting to ever let go.

"Mom, I promise that I will call you every day, and if you ever need me, you have to promise me that you'll let me know."

"I will . . ."

"And I will come home anytime you need me."

"Zoe, call them back and tell them that you accept the position."

I hugged her again and then ran to the telephone. I accepted the position, on the condition that I could spend a few more days in Miami with my mother. It seemed that Douglas Ware was happy to have me any way he could. He agreed to give me a week.

My mother and I maximized our time together, taking walks to the park, watching television together and, most of the time, just talking. We talked through old memories that were painful to both of us, yet they became less so after we'd brought them into the open.

"Baby, Mama's sorry I had my attention on all those men, instead of you and your brother. I just got so caught up with them drugs and stuff. I felt like nothin', and them men and them drugs . . . They made me feel like something. I ain't had no good job. No husband. But now, I realize I was a foolish woman. I had two beautiful children. Y'all's love could have carried me through."

Hearing those words of repentence warmed my heart like a cup of hot soup. We just hugged. I knew at that moment my mom meant so much to me.

On the morning that I was to leave, I stood in the bathroom and stared in the mirror. I couldn't believe that seven days had passed since I accepted the position, and I prayed that I was doing the right thing—leaving my mother. But inside, I felt a peace that I hadn't felt in a long time. And I knew this came from God.

My mother held my hand as we walked to my car for the final time. When I got into the car, Mom stroked my cheek and gave me some parting words of wisdom.

"God chose two different roads for us, Zoe. I'm so grateful for the time we've been able to spend together. Now we're entering a season where we won't be together all the time. But I'll pray for you every day."

I nodded, not wanting to cry. "I'll pray for you too, Mom."

She smiled. "I know you will, and in those prayers, we'll be together." She gave me a final hug. "I am so proud of you," she whispered.

Once I pulled away, the tears began to flow. And I cried all the way to the airport.

I called Shay as soon as the plane landed in Seattle. She was thrilled that I had returned and was happy to let me stay with her. Her wedding was still more than a month away, and that was more than enough time for me to find a place of my own.

"Please don't tell Chase I'm back," I begged her that night, once I was settled into her guest bedroom.

She frowned. "I think it's stupid of you to try to hide from him. But if that's what you really want . . ."

"It is," I assured her. "I don't want him to be my focus. I'm going to try to walk in the Spirit, not in the flesh."

"Okay," Shay said, agreeing to abide by my wishes.

"So, how's the Seattle Storm doing?" I asked.

Her eyes widened. "Don't tell me you haven't been following the team!"

I shrugged. "Been too busy," I said.

She shook her head. "Well, it looks like we're in the hunt for the playoffs. We've been winning! And you know that Chase has been doing it. He's definitely the man."

Though I couldn't bring myself to see Chase, or even call him, I was glad to hear things were going well for him.

The next morning, I arrived at the Seattle Storm headquarters thirty minutes before I was expected. Douglas Ware was already there and showed me to my cubicle.

"I hate to throw you in right away," Mr. Ware said. "But we have so much to do. First, the Christmas party." He reviewed the details they had so far. "Now, feel free to come up with whatever strategy you think best, Zoe— theme, place, menu—all the stuff that will make the evening a memorable one."

"You got it," I said, thrilled to have the opportunity to dig in right away and show him what I could do. "I've got some great ideas. We can make it a charity ball."

"Sounds good. You're thinking. I like that. I also need you to take responsibility for the players' public appearances," he added, dropping a folder on my desk. "Here are just a few of the requests we've been getting. Now, depending on your schedule, it would be nice if you could accompany the players to some of the events, to make sure things go off without a hitch."

"Sure. Okay," I said, praying that Chase wasn't scheduled for anything soon.

"One of the players is scheduled to visit a children's home this afternoon," Mr. Ware continued. "Maybe you should go along." Before I could answer, he looked up. "Chase! Hey, buddy!" Mr. Ware stepped out of my cubicle.

I remained in my chair, out of Chase's view. My heart pounded and all kinds of thoughts raced through my mind. *Do I look okay? Has Chase been thinking about me? What is he going to say when he sees me?*

I took a deep breath. *Lord, I really wanted to avoid this guy, but You brought him to me. Help me know what to say to him.*

"Hey, thanks for agreeing to go to the children's home," Mr. Ware said, standing just outside my cubicle. "I know you've been real busy, but it really means a lot to the organization that you would represent us with this charity." Mr. Ware stepped back into my cubicle. "Chase, I'd like you to meet the new person who'll be handling appearances for us. This is Zoe Clarke."

I stood. The sight of Chase took my breath away, and my knees nearly melted. The man looked even finer than I remembered. I reached out my hand to shake his, trying to keep it from trembling. Instead of taking my hand, he reached out and hugged me.

I almost collapsed from relief. I was glad he didn't feel the need to be formal. A hug was definitely more appropriate between us. We'd been through too much for a dull, ordinary handshake. Just two weeks before, he had been my man. I was glad he still cared enough to let me know I still meant something.

"I take it you two know each other?" Mr. Ware asked.

Before Chase could tell it all, as I could see he was about to do, I interjected, "Yes, sir, we went to college together at the University of Miami."

Taking my lead, Chase allowed the rest of the conversation to remain professional.

"Well, if you have a moment, Chase," Mr. Ware said, "I'd like to go over the appearance for this afternoon." He turned to me. "Zoe, would you join us?"

I nodded and followed the two men into the conference room. As Mr. Ware gave us the details for this afternoon's appearance, my mind wandered.

I began to wonder what would happen with Chase and me. I wanted to ask him out. We needed to talk. I ached to ask for his forgiveness, and judging from the hug, I could tell he missed me.

But when Mr. Ware finished and stood to leave, I lost my nerve.

Chase said, "Well, Zoe, it was nice to see you again. Will I see you at the children's home?"

"I'm not sure," I answered. "I'm going to try, but it depends on what Mr. Ware has going on for me."

"Okay," he said casually. "Well, I hope you can make it. See ya later." Then he left and I slowly returned to my solitary desk.

From the moment I walked into the children's home, I was sad. It seemed to be a lonely place. My childhood hadn't been the greatest—living among roaches, not being able to connect with my mother, my father dying when I was so young; often we barely had enough food on the table. But this place made my circumstances almost look like heaven. The biggest difference between how I grew up and this home was that with all I went through, I always believed that my parents loved me.

This facility was plain, cold and clean, reminding me of a hospital. As I stared into the children's eyes, I saw the same thing: coldness. They didn't look at all happy. Their eyes held no hope. But then, I asked myself, why should they be hopeful? These were older children and there was very little chance of them ever leaving this place with adoptive parents.

I introduced myself to the administrator, who shook my hand quickly and looked past me to Chase.

"Mr. Farr, we are so excited to have you here today," she fawned. "Thank you so much for coming."

I wanted to gag the way she threw herself at him, but I just smiled as I took a seat in the front row of the auditorium.

I smiled at Chase as he sat on the stage with workers from the home. When the administrator introduced Chase and he stood, the boys and girls, ranging in age from seven to seventeen, barely applauded. But by the time he was halfway through his speech, they were sitting on the edge of their seats. I watched in awe as Chase encouraged those kids.

"Even though you don't have parents around," he said, "you have one parent who is always with you. You have a heavenly Father who is providing for you, even now. At least you're not living on the streets. Here you have workers who love you and take care of you. You know, God has a purpose and a plan for each and every one of you, and all of you are very important to Him."

I looked at the children's faces and watched as the despair in their eyes turned to hope. It made me smile. I felt good inside for being a part of it.

Chase glanced at me as he spoke and I smiled and nodded. What he was doing here was greater than catching passes and scoring touchdowns. He was winning little souls for Christ.

"Well, now it's time for me to go." Chase began to end his speech. "But before I do, I want to introduce you to someone."

The children sat quietly in anticipation and I blushed, thrilled that he was going to give me a special introduction.

"Kids, I'd like you to meet a very special lady. Her name is Waverly Phillips. She's one of the Storm's cheerleaders."

The children burst into applause and a bouncy blond bimbo-looking chick, who had been sitting beside Chase, stood and gave a big, toothy grin. I'd noticed the girl, of course, but had figured she was one of the children's home workers. She wasn't wearing a cheerleader uniform, and Mr. Ware hadn't mentioned anything about a cheerleader accompanying us.

I crossed my arms and wondered what she was doing here . . . and was she with Chase? As far as I was concerned, if she wasn't in uniform, she wasn't representing the Storm.

I didn't know any of the cheerleaders by face. I'd seen them at the home games but had never gotten close enough to recognize any of them. But for some reason, this one's name rang a bell.

Waverly Phillips. Why did I know that name?

Then it hit me! This was the chick who had left a message on the answering machine the night of the big hailstorm. The one he had given a ride home to after the away game.

Waverly stood next to Chase at the podium.

"I am so glad to be here," she gushed. "It is so neat to be a Storm cheerleader."

She *sounded* like a bimbo too. But Chase didn't seem to think so. I watched his eyes as he watched her. He seemed intrigued and impressed, though I didn't know why. I wasn't impressed at all.

I decided right then that I was going to have to break down and speak to Chase . . . and soon. I didn't want whatever was going on with this cheerleader babe to go any further. But then again, why was I deluding myself. I was not in any postion to dictate to him what he should do?

When Chase and Waverly finally stepped away from the podium, I stood, eager to go to Chase. But a little girl with braids and a droopy brown face stopped me in my tracks.

"Do you think I'm pretty?" she asked with puppy dog eyes.

"Yes," I said, deciding my talk with Chase could wait. I sat down in a small chair beside her. "Why would you ask me that?"

"Because I want to be pretty like you when I grow up. And if I'm not pretty now, I won't be pretty later. Nobody here thinks I'm pretty."

"Oh, that's not true at all. You're very pretty."

The girl lowered her eyes. "Before I got sent here, my foster mama told me I was the ugliest thing she had ever seen." She looked down at her hands and spoke softly. "Sometimes, when I look in the mirror, I think she's right."

"What's your name?" I asked the girl.

"Kiana."

"My, what a beautiful name. Kiana, let me look at you."
She slowly lifted her face. "Oh, sweetie, your foster mom
was way wrong. You are beautiful."

"Really?" Her face lit up, her big, toothy smile making
her look heavenly.

"Absolutely. And what's more important, you're lovely
on the inside too. That's the best beauty in the whole
world. God don't make no junk, Kiana. I bet when you
grow up, you're gonna be much prettier than me."

Her smile grew even wider, and she gave me a tight hug.
As I hugged her back, I prayed, *Lord, continue to give this girl
hope.*

Kiana released me. "Thank you," she said before she hurried off with some other girls.

I stood and made my way to Chase.

"I'm so glad you made it," he said. But a second later,
Little Miss Cheerleader saw us talking, and she joined us.
"Zoe," Chase said, "I'd like to introduce you to Waverly.
Waverly, Zoe works in the public-relations office for the
Storm."

What? My mind reeled. *He couldn't possibly have just introduced me as an office person! I am his girl. Why doesn't he tell
her that?*

"Well, hi, Zoe," Waverly bubbled. "It's so great to meet
you."

"Mr. Ware didn't tell me there were going to be cheerleaders at this event," I said, not caring that I sounded harsh.

"Oh, I didn't have to come this afternoon." She smiled
again. I wondered if her lips hurt from pasting on that

goofy grin all the time. "I like doing things like this, and Chase told me he was coming, so I figured I'd tag along. Anything I can do to give back to the community, I'll do. And spending more time with Chase is always a plus."

"I see. So, you and Chase spend a lot of time together?" I wondered what Chase was thinking about the edge in my voice. But I didn't take my eyes off her big baby blues.

"Oh, yes." Waverly giggled, oblivious to the sarcasm that dripped from my words. "We've been dating for almost a week now, and things have just been great." She shot a glance at Chase. "Well, I guess I shouldn't call it dating." I felt a brief surge of relief. "Technically, players and cheerleaders aren't supposed to date."

My heart sank to my knees.

"Besides," she went on, clueless of my pain, "Chase is so busy, I'll take whatever time I can spend with him." She kept going on telling me her business. It was strange because she didn't even know me.

I stood frozen. Although I made sure that I didn't show it on the outside, tears were choking my heart. Chase and I had been apart for just two weeks, and he was already dating? And a white chick, no less. I didn't have any problem with interracial relationships, but I remembered him dating a white girl in college, and he said she was a big phony. This Waverly chick seemed pretty phony to me.

Besides, Chase was supposed to be in love with me. This cheerleader babe could have been green-skinned with purple hair and I would have disliked her just as much. All the hopes I had of getting back with Chase disappeared. I'd thought he still felt something for me. I realized, now, that

I had secretly hoped as soon as he knew I was back in town, we'd automatically get back together.

But he was obviously into this girl now. My heart buried itself deep within my chest, and I wasn't sure it would ever come out again.

There was no doubt that I loved this man, but I'd just have to get over it. Chase had moved on. The bright future I had hoped might still be possible for Chase and me wasn't going to happen. The forecast of a sunny day was no longer accurate. I was really going to have to trust God, because all I could see was a hazy overcast.

Chapter 12

Looking at Chase standing beside Waverly made my body tremble. The way he looked at her was identical to the way he'd looked at me just fourteen days before. But I was no longer his leading lady. And it was my fault.

Waverly caressed my man's back.

Yeah, I knew we had split up. But I felt he still belonged to me. And yet, I couldn't say or do anything. I couldn't tell her to move her hand. I couldn't tell her to back off. I couldn't say, *Excuse me, but this is not your merchandise.*

Inside, I prayed. I wanted and needed to let the Holy Spirit guide me. I needed God's help in controlling the jealous monster inside me that wanted to rip Waverly's hair out.

Waverly continued jabbering, telling me all about her "dates" with Chase, and I finally couldn't take it anymore. I gave Chase a sad look; then I grabbed my purse and my folder and headed for the exit.

But the door was so heavy, I couldn't open the stupid thing with my hands full. I pushed hard, and the papers in my folder fell to the ground. I muttered under my breath.

Like a knight in shining armor, Chase appeared beside me. He knelt and helped me pick up the papers that had fluttered onto the floor. I didn't know whether to be thankful or angry.

"I got it," I lied, even though I really wanted his help.

He ignored me and lifted the papers anyway. We both stood at the same time. Chase opened the door. When we stepped outside, he asked, "Are you okay?"

"What do you think?" I snapped. "We've only been apart a couple of weeks and you're already dating!"

"You disappeared, Zoe. You didn't call. Didn't even leave a forwarding number. Did you expect my life to stop?"

"No," I admitted, some of the attitude gone from my voice. "But I didn't expect your love for me to end so fast. If what we had was real, how could you quit loving me so quickly?"

"Who said I didn't love you anymore?" he whispered. "Zoe, Waverly and I are friends. She'd like it to be more, but it's not. You and I have issues that—"

"Issues? Go ahead and say it. I'm the reason we're apart."

He hesitated for a moment before he nodded. "That's true."

"Geez, Chase. You waited almost four years for me. You couldn't wait two more weeks? You wanted me the whole time I was having sex with Devyn, but then when I wanted to have sex with you, you couldn't handle it?"

"It was more than that, Zoe. You knew where I stood."

I was hot and ready to tell Chase everything that I believed. "And do you think it will be any different with that white chick in there? Believe me, she is gonna want a piece of you. Remember college? Those white girls just wanted the pro-bound athletes. They didn't want the regular brotha's. Don't think she likes you because you're nice. You *are* the Storm, Chase. She only wants one thing—to lock you in bed so she can lock onto your wallet."

Chase's face began to turn red. "Do you think I'm that naive?"

"If you can't see her real motives, then, yeah, I do think you're naive."

I tried to stop the tears that threatened to flow from my eyes, but my emotions were high. Still, I was determined to finish having my say.

"You know, I'm glad we didn't sleep together. Now, that's one less thing I have to worry about. Here, I've been all bummed out because I wanted to express what I felt for you in the deepest way I knew how. Thank God He stopped that. He knew I didn't need to be hurt like that twice."

I could tell my words weren't accomplishing anything. Chase's eyes darted toward the door every few minutes, obviously checking for Waverly. Did he think I was stupid, that I didn't see and understand what he was doing?

"You know what?" I said, ignoring his wandering eyes. "It's not even an issue anymore. Do whatever you want to do. I've got a job in the office, and you work on the field. We don't ever have to see each other. Go ahead and finish up with the kids here, do your civic duty, then head out on your date or whatever you want to call it. I just don't care anymore." Without waiting for a response, I rushed off. And I didn't turn back, even though I could feel Chase's eyes following me.

*   *   *

"There you are," Shay said as I entered the bridal boutique. "Where have you been?"

"The world doesn't revolve around you, Shay," I mumbled.

"What?"

"I'm sorry I'm late," I said, changing my tone. "You look beautiful." I didn't know how many gowns she'd tried on before I arrived. I'd gotten so caught up with Chase that I'd almost forgotten about my promise to meet her at the boutique.

As I looked at her in the elegant silk gown, a stab of pain squeezed my heart like a vise. I remembered my own botched wedding day and the way my gorgeous white dress had turned muddy brown by the end of the night.

Though I knew why God didn't want me to be with Devyn, I remembered now all of the high hopes I'd had for us. I was surprised to find myself wondering how Devyn was doing. I wondered what he was doing now. And I wondered how far along Aisha was and if they were still together.

It didn't make sense—all the questions I had. I guess seeing Chase, especially with another girl, started me to think about my ex. I knew it wasn't healthy, but I couldn't help fantasizing.

"Do you really like it?" Shay said, pulling me away from my thoughts of Devyn.

"Yeah, it's perfect," I said without really looking.

"Seriously, do you absolutely love it?" Shay twirled so that I could see her from every angle. "You know I want to be the most beautiful person in the world on my special day."

"The dress looks adorable," I assured her, finally looking at her. "But don't ask me. Whatever gown you want is the one I want for you."

Shay pouted. "That's not very helpful."

"Look, why do we have to go through all this drama?"

"You sure are putting a damper on things. I've been waiting for you to get here so I could show you some of my favorite dresses, and now you're totally spoiling it. What's wrong with you?"

I wanted to be angry at Shay, but she was right. I was moping, having a pity party. I was jealous. I wanted to be the happy bride. Shay had a Christian man who cared for her and I had no man. Not that I needed one. I knew God had to be the center of my life first. But a little bit of the flesh was starting to take over.

"All right," I said, trying to sound cheerful. I smiled. "Show me the rest of the dresses you like."

Shay led me back to the huge dressing area and I helped her unzip the gown.

"Really, Zoe," she asked, "what's going on?"

I sighed. "I just saw Chase at an event and he's dating another girl. I was gone for only two weeks; he never tried to get in touch with me and now he's with somebody else."

"Oh, Zoe, he wanted to call you," Shay said as she stepped out of her dress.

I frowned. "How do you know?"

"He asked me for your number."

My eyes opened wide. "He did?"

"Yeah." Shay placed the gown on the hanger. "He called me, like, three times asking where you were."

"What did you tell him?" I held my breath.

"I told him exactly what you told me to say. That you didn't want to talk to him. That it was over between you two. That he needed to move on and not try to track you down."

I groaned. "Why'd you tell him that?"

"That's what you told me to say. You made me promise."

I slumped onto the dressing-room bench. "I didn't really mean it. Couldn't you have told him that I missed him?"

Shay parked her hands on her tiny hips. "Like I'm supposed to read your mind? I don't know you *that* well. I did what you told me because I didn't want to get you angry. You were adamant when you left."

"I know, but . . . ." I shook my head.

Shay sighed. "I'm sorry if I did the wrong thing, Zoe, but I honored your wishes. It just wasn't my place to tell Chase something different."

"I'm sorry, Shay. You're right. But what am I going to do now?" I felt like crying. "Chase is with somebody else, and he thinks that I don't even want to talk to him." I left the dressing area, shaking with frustration. The raging winds of despair were attacking me from every side.

I knew that I had no right to blame Shay for telling Chase exactly what I asked her to say. How could I have been so unfair? I was trying to start an argument, blame it all on her. It suddenly occurred to me that maybe all the girlfriend drama I'd experienced in the past was at least partly my fault.

Even with Tasha. Though I knew that she had told just about everyone we knew in Miami about my troubles, maybe that was partly my fault. Maybe I had made her jealous in some way. My mother had told me that Tasha was telling people that I got what I deserved. Well, I didn't deserve the humiliation, but in this situation with Chase, maybe I was getting what I deserved. I had told Shay what to say and she had said it, and now I had to live with the consequences.

I returned to the dressing room. Shay was sitting in one of the velvet chairs, clad only in her underwear, her head lowered in her hands. When she looked up, her eyes were red.

"I didn't mean to break you and Chase up," she cried.

I hoped that my smile would cheer her up and change the mood.

"Let's not talk about this anymore. You've got a wedding to think about, and I'm not serving you the way I should." I sat in the chair next to her. "I've got a lot of issues right now, but I shouldn't be putting that on you. Come on now, show me another one of those dresses."

Shay searched my eyes and then hugged me before she reached for a second dress. I helped her slip into the gown.

"You know," I said, fastening the row of pearl buttons that lined the back, "I believe God's trying to teach me something."

"What?" she asked.

"It's all about storms," I said, thinking about that Max Lucado book the girl on the plane had sent me. "My ruined wedding was a terrible storm, and it took me a long time to get over it. But every time I make it through one storm, it starts raining again, and the next thing you know, I'm going through more lightning and thunder. Seeing Chase with another girl was just the latest crazy storm God's allowed into my life."

Shay placed her hands on my arms. "You need to get a better perspective, Zoe. God has given you a great new job. And even though Chase seems to be dating somebody else right now, I know God's gonna work that out too." She grinned at me. "He's told Byron several times that he misses you," she whispered as if she were telling me a secret.

I wished I could believe her, but I shook my head. "You didn't see him today," I said sadly. "I really think he's moving on. But, once again, I'm the one to blame." I stepped back and looked at Shay in the new dress. "But, hey, enough about me. You are going to be a beautiful Christmas bride." I smiled, thinking about how Shay and Byron had decided to marry at midnight on Christmas Eve.

"Thanks," she said. "And don't worry. Your day is coming too."

We embraced again. It had been a while since I felt good about girlfriend interaction. The moment meant a lot to me. I had lashed out at her, yet she gave me grace. The same kind of grace God gave me daily. I knew I needed to do my part.

I stepped back and eyed her in the dress. "You know, I like this one better than the first. But you'll look good in any of them. Okay, put on the next one," I said, taking another dress from the rack. "Let's take a look."

Shay took one last look at herself in the mirror and then began to slip from her dress. We chatted as she tried on dress after dress. And, by the end of the day, I had almost forgotten about my troubles and was beginning to be very excited about Shay's big day.

For the next two days, I sat in my cubicle answering one phone request after another for the new Storm star, Chase Farr. It seemed as if every organization in Seattle wanted him to appear at its functions. I was proud of him, but I was also getting tired of feeling like his personal secretary.

But that wasn't the only thing getting on my nerves. I was sick of hearing people chat about their Thanksgiving plans. It wasn't like I had anywhere to go or anyone special to spend the day with.

Shay had invited me to spend the holiday with her and Byron, but I couldn't stand the thought of watching them be all romantic with each other. It would just remind me of what I didn't have, and I didn't want to go there.

Late Wednesday afternoon, the day before Thanksgiving, I was about to leave the office when the phone rang again.

Lord, I prayed, *please don't let this be another phone call about Chase!*

The moment I picked up the phone and heard my brother's voice, I remembered the cliché that said you had to be careful what you prayed for.

Shock waves jolted through me when Alonzo said, "Zoe, can you talk?"

"It's Mom, isn't it?" I asked, barely able to get the words through my throat.

"Her cancer came back," Alonzo said. "But this time, it's in her brain."

"Oh, no." My body turned to jelly and I fell into my chair.

"You need to get home right away," my brother insisted. "She's asking for you."

Weeks earlier, if I had received this phone call, I would have asked, *Lord, why?* And though I certainly didn't want this to be the end of my mom's life journey, I was now at a place where I wanted her to be at peace. I was just thankful that God had allowed me time with my mother to talk through so many of our issues and for me to finally know what an awesome mother I had.

"How is she feeling?" I asked Alonzo.

"She's really frail and weak, Zoe. Her eyes are red and swollen. I can practically see her bones. Though she tries not to complain, she's in constant pain. She can't stop moaning."

"Alonzo, I'll be home as soon as I can. I'll keep you posted about my arrangements."

I wasted no time rushing to Mr. Ware's office and explaining that I needed some time off.

"I understand this is awfully soon since I just started. If you need to replace me, Mr. Ware, I understand. But I have to go to my mother."

"Of course you do," my boss said with empathy. "You take as much time as you need. We'll muddle through until you get back."

I thanked him profusely. "I promise that when I get back I will get everything under control."

"You know, you'll be hard-pressed to find an open seat on any flights tonight," he warned. "With it being Thanksgiving."

My heart sank. I hadn't thought about that.

Mr. Ware must have seen the distress in my eyes. "You know what? Let me see if I can arrange a private charter for you. I'll call the team's pilot."

I couldn't believe Mr. Ware was doing this amazing thing for me, and I could see God's hands all over this. I thanked God for such an incredible boss and for the blessing He was giving me.

That night, I was on a shuttle from Seattle to Miami and I thought about my mother the entire cross-country trip.

It was bittersweet that my mother and I had just arrived at this place where we could have a good relationship. For so many years, I'd carried so much baggage, resenting everything about my mother, especially the way she lived. I blamed many of my problems on her and the way I was raised. I blamed her for my promiscuity. The way she had men in and out of our apartment all the time. Loving them so that they could put dinner on the table. I had watched her please men with her body, so I grew up thinking that was the only way to keep a man.

But there was no blame to be placed. My mother did what she had to do, what she thought was right at the time. She had made her peace with God and I was so glad that I had made my peace with her. God had extended His grace to both my mother and me. And I was learning to extend grace to my mother.

The sun was rising in Miami when Alonzo let me into my mother's apartment and I walked into her bedroom. She tried to smile and held out a thin, frail arm to me. Just lifting her arm off the bed seemed to be a struggle. I clasped her cold hand tightly and buried my face into her bosom.

"Oh, baby," she said in a weak voice. "Don't cry."

When I looked up again, I couldn't believe how she had deteriorated since I'd last seen her. It wasn't fair. "Mom, as I was flying here, I never questioned God for a minute. But this isn't right."

"I'm really tired, Zoe." Mom spoke with the wistful sound of a tired saint. "But I'm excited about what's yet to come for me. I feel ready for heaven." Although her words were difficult to accept, they sounded like sweet music. It seemed the Holy Spirit was speaking. God had given her Himself.

"When I hear that trumpet sound," my mother continued, her eyes glassy and unfocused, "I'm going up yonder to be with my Lord." She turned and looked at me. "But first, I get to tell you how sorry I am that I wasn't the kind of mother I should have been."

"Mom, you don't have to say that anymore. We already talked about it and I forgive you, just like I hope that you've forgiven me."

My mother tried to smile. "I don't have anything to forgive you for. You've been the perfect daughter."

I shook my head, but I couldn't speak.

My mother said, "I am proud of the way you turned out. Zoe, you're more wonderful than I ever hoped."

"Oh, Mom," I said through my tears, "I'm far from perfect."

"But just look at you. You went to college. You got a good job. You're beautiful, talented, strong."

"I don't feel very strong right now," I whimpered.

"That's all right. The Lord's gonna do something great with you in His time. He's just using this cold winter season of your life to get you ready."

I was surprised at what she said. *Winter.* That was exactly what I felt like I was going through, a winter in my emotions. "What do you think God is trying to prepare me for?"

"For whatever He has planned for you to do, my girl. And don't worry. You won't have to do it alone. God told me He's sending you a good man."

I sniffed. "I'm afraid I've already blown God's blessing in that area."

"Zoe, if I would have known the Lord in my twenties, like you, my life would have been so much more fulfilling. If only I had known what He called me to do and done it earlier!" She paused and coughed.

I knew it was difficult for her to talk, but she was determined to continue.

"Now, 'cause of my illness, I got church folks and neighbors from the projects all coming by to see me. And I been talkin' to 'em all about the Lord and witnessin' to 'em. I been able to tell 'em that they gotta know Christ. I'm witnessin' more from here in this bed than in all the rest of my years on this earth. I've even been helpin' some folks get saved, Zoe! God has been using my last days to make sure other people have endless days. I'm so thankful. I don't deserve to be used." I squeezed her hand tighter. "My life has been nothin' but drama. But I can truly say that at the end I've had peace." She squeezed my hand. "Find out what God wants you to do, Zoe, and just do it. Be ready when He calls."

My tears fell onto the paper-thin skin of her hand. "Oh, Mom, I can't stand the thought of losing you."

"You're not losing me, baby. The connection we have through Jesus will go on forever."

I pressed my lips against her fingers. "I love you, Mommy."

"I love you too, baby. Always know that."

I laid my head on her chest and rested.

I spent the entire day with my mother and brother, but we didn't celebrate Thanksgiving in the traditional way. We ordered a pizza and spent our time just talking, bonding and using the time that God was giving us to get closer.

"Hey, Zoe, isn't the Storm playing today?" Alonzo asked at one point.

I glanced at the television but didn't have any interest in turning it on. I shrugged and Alonzo let the subject drop.

That night, I helped Alonzo tuck Mom into bed.

"Mom, would you like me to stay in here with you?"

She smiled. "I'd like that," she said before closing her eyes.

My plan had been to just stay until my mother fell asleep, but when I took her hand in mine and laid my head on her chest, I fell asleep to the soft rising of her chest.

It was after three in the morning when I woke up. I looked at my mother; she was smiling in her sleep. I leaned over to kiss her and her cheek felt cold.

My heart began to pound. I felt her hand. Cold. I touched her forehead. Cold.

Slowly, I backed out of the room and woke up Alonzo, who was sleeping on the couch.

Without words, he jumped up and ran into Mom's room. I paced in the living room, fighting to hold back my tears. When Alonzo came out and held me, I finally admitted the truth: My mother was gone.

I walked through the next days in a fog, smiling at the people who came by to express their condolences, making arrangements as if it were part of my job, helping my brother divide up Mom's few personal possessions, most of which we were going to donate to charity.

It was only when I was alone at night that I released my pain into my pillow, crying tears of sorrow for the years I'd wasted blaming my mother for my life. But I was also releasing tears of joy for being closer to my mother and having been with her when she took her last breath.

On Sunday when I awakened, I prayed that the Lord would give me strength to get through the day—that He would provide a way for me to say my final good-bye to my mother.

The church was frigid, even though it was packed with people. Alonzo and I held hands as we marched into the church past all of the others who had come to pay their last respects. Although I could feel everyone looking at me, I kept my eyes straight ahead—looking at the front of the church. Looking at the casket that held my mother.

When Alonzo and I got to the front, he squeezed my hand tighter. I knew he was worried about me, but I smiled at him, letting my brother know that I was all right.

I looked down at my mother lying in the casket, cold and still. She looked at peace. It was as if I could see Jesus holding her.

As I kissed her forehead, I felt like I was in a valley and I was too weak to make the climb out. Tears rippled down my face, and I nearly collapsed. My brother did his best to hold me up. Uncles and aunts surrounded me as I made my way back to the pew.

It was good to know my mother was with the Lord, but I felt abandoned. My heart was caught in a churning funnel cloud of despair. I had to find some joy. Mom wasn't suffering anymore, and someday I knew I would join her. In the end, she'd found Christ. That alone was enough to make me shout, *Hallelujah!*

As the pastor spoke, I rejoiced for my mom. But I felt sorry for myself. My mother wasn't coming back. We had finally found a connection and now there was no opportunity to grow closer. Even though I knew she was better off, I felt devastated.

My cousin Ray stood and sang a song called "Anchored in the Lord." It was a testament to my mother's life, and to mine as well. His voice sounded heavenly. God knew I needed to hear that song.

My mom had suffered through more strife than I ever would. And yet, in the end, she had hope. She knew that if she didn't wake up on this side of heaven again, she would be going to a special place that God had prepared. Her struggles didn't stop until the very end, but her precious soul was anchored in the Lord.

Pastor Paul Porcher took the podium. "Sister Clarke lived her last days in a way that let others know Christ is the way," he said in his soothing preacher's voice. "She used every opportunity to talk about God and the amazing things He had done for her. And for any of you who didn't get a chance to hear her tell her story, she wanted me to tell you about the One who saved her, and who can save you too. The Lord can clear up any troubles that come in your life. Sometimes that very trouble is what makes us draw near to Him. He's knocking on your door right now, people. If you put your ear close enough to the door and stay real quiet, you can hear Him."

"Preach on!" somebody called from the back.

"But if you keep doing the things of the world, if you keep living crazy, He's gonna have to bang down the door and make you get it. Now, while there's sunshine in your life, is the time to praise God. Not for what you don't have, but for what He's already given you!"

"Amen," said another mourner.

"Know that you are nothing without Him. When the whirlwind comes and rips your world apart, it'll make your day turn into unending night. If that night comes too quickly, if it turns so dark that the wave encompasses your calm beach, you might be taken into the water, where you'll suffocate and drown and find yourself in hell eternally."

I imagined my mom smiling at the pastor's analogy. The thought made me smile a bit too.

"Sister Clarke found Jesus in her last hours. Hallelujah! Now she's been rewarded with the ultimate prize, the ultimate joy, the ultimate peace. And God wants to give that same peace to each one of you."

Pastor Paul Porcher called for those who didn't know the Lord to come to the altar. I watched as he held his hand forward, inviting people to join him at the altar. Slowly, people stood, one by one, and made their way to the front of the church. Within moments, thirteen people stood around my mother's shiny black coffin. And minutes later, they prayed the Sinner's Prayer with Pastor Porcher and accepted Christ.

A tear of joy trickled down my face. Even in death, my mother was doing the same thing she'd done during her last days on earth—winning souls for Christ. How marvelous.

As we filed out of the sanctuary, the faces around me blurred. My eyes were awash with tears. When I got to the door and saw my mom's casket being loaded into the hearse, I lost my balance. Someone caught me, saving me from falling to the ground.

I turned to thank my rescuer and found myself staring into the face of my ex.

"I'm so sorry, sweetheart," Devyn said, still holding me.

"Devyn!" I cried out. "Thank you so much for being here today."

I didn't know how he'd found out, how he knew I needed him to be there. But his presence comforted me. It filled a deep emotional void.

"I don't know what you're doing afterward," he said, looking around as if he were unsure that he should be speaking.

I shook my head. "Just going back to my mom's."

"I'll meet you over there." He kissed my cheek.

I knew that there were many watching, wondering and whispering. But I didn't care. It felt good to have Devyn there. It felt good to have someone to lean on.

After we returned from the cemetery, Devyn drew me away from the lingering mourners and took me to his apartment.

"I just want to help you in any way that I can, Zoe," he said, touching my face softly and leading me to a room in the back. "Whatever I can do for you, I will do."

As Devyn gazed into my weary, red eyes, I realized that I was alone with him in his bedroom. I couldn't believe I was here—never did I imagine this. And I was sure Aisha, wherever she was, couldn't imagine this either.

Yet, there we stood, eyeing each other. I was vulnerable. Staring at his gorgeous body, I desperately wanted him to comfort me physically. I had lost so much of myself that day. I needed something to reassure me that I was still alive. I melted into his warm embrace. Was this how my mother had felt in the long, lonely years after my father died? Had she wanted comfort from a man's embrace?

"I know this has been difficult for you," he said as he eased me toward the bed. "But I don't want you to think about any of that right now. I just want you to remember how it used to be with us. How good it used to feel. I want to make you feel good again, sweetheart." He gently placed his lips against mine.

I pulled back. "What about Aisha? And your baby?"

Devyn rubbed my tired arms. "That baby ain't mine, Zoe. You were right about that girl. She is crazy. I made a big mistake choosing her over you." His hands moved to my face. "You're the one who made me everything I am. You helped me reach my goals. All Aisha wanted was to get into my pockets, sit at home and live off me with another man's kid."

Devyn kissed my neck, my forehead, my nose, then worked his tongue into my mouth. The kiss felt so familiar, and I suddenly realized how much I had missed it. I responded. Our tongues fell into a rhythmic flow as they twirled around each other.

He unbuttoned my blouse and then placed my hands on his fly. I knew what he wanted me to do. I pulled down the zipper in one deft, well-practiced move.

Before I knew it, we were standing, wearing only our underwear. As we embraced, I felt revived. Oh, how I had missed his touch. The thought of pleasing him physically engulfed my mind. In that moment of hot passion, I was caught up in a whirlwind. It was a crazy, sexy love typhoon.

Chapter 13

As Devyn slipped my bra strap over my shoulder, the good feeling started to bother me. His sensuous kisses became irritating.

All of a sudden, I wanted him away from me. "Stop!" I yelled, wondering what I had been thinking. "I can't do this. I don't love you. I don't want you."

He looked at me, but only for a moment before he tried to cover my mouth with his. I pushed him away. Now I knew how Chase had felt when I had pushed myself on him.

"Come on, babe. Let me make you feel good." It was as if he were ignoring my words.

I pulled up my bra strap. "I'm sorry, Devyn."

As I put my blouse back on and buttoned it, Devyn continued to try to convince me. "Look, I know you had a thing with Chase, but he's a big football star now. He can get some anywhere. I'm sure you ain't nowhere in his thoughts."

I looked at Devyn as if he were crazy. I wanted to slap that boy. Tell him to shut up. Tell him he didn't know what he was talking about. But his words sounded too close to the truth. Chase probably wasn't thinking of me.

I pulled on my stockings, praying for strength. Praying for the Lord to come to me and help me understand all of this.

It worked, because I suddenly realized that it wasn't sex I needed to make me feel whole. It wasn't Devyn or Chase. I needed to be happy with me because I was a child of God, not somebody's girlfriend. I longed for the deep, abiding pleasure of God's Word, not the temporary pleasure of sin.

I looked around for my skirt and found it draped over the back of the headboard. As I reached for it, I heard the front door open and slam into a wall.

"Devyn! Where are you?"

Oh, great! I thought at the sound of Aisha's voice. I struggled into my skirt.

"You best not have that wench in here," Aisha screamed, her footsteps stomping closer. "I done heard you was comforting her at her mama's funeral, but she better not be in my house!"

With a cocky grin, Devyn opened the bedroom door. He was still only dressed in his underwear.

Aisha stood in the doorway, her tummy bulging under a maternity top that hugged her middle. She glared at Devyn, then turned her eyes to me. Before I could do anything, she flew at me like a maniac. She had me pinned up against the wall, her hands gripping my neck.

"I'm gonna kill you for messin' wit' my man."

Aisha was sweating profusely. She had to be on something—speed, heroin, crack. I wasn't sure. I managed to squeeze away from her grasp and searched desperately for my shoes. I noticed them halfway under the bed, and lunged for them. When I stood up, shoes in hand, Aisha pulled a 9mm pistol from her purse and aimed it at me with shaky hands.

"Aisha, put that gun down!" Devyn shouted, positioning himself between this crazy woman and me.

"Don't tell me what to do, boy. You just step back. I'm gonna shoot you too before I let you be with another!" She wagged the gun in his face.

With her focus on him, I dashed for the phone. Before I could dial, she growled, "Don't even think about it!" Her red-rimmed eyes glared at me like a wild animal's.

I felt like I was in the middle of a movie. This chick was about to shoot me over Devyn, and I didn't even want him. Maybe if I told her that, she'd let me go. But I knew the drugs in her system probably wouldn't allow her really to hear me.

The wild woman shoved past Devyn and pressed the pistol against my temple, forcing my head back.

"Aisha," I mumbled, "I just lost my mom."

"Yeah, and you about to join her," she said as she cocked the hammer.

I closed my eyes and sent up a quick, panicked prayer. *Lord, help me, please. I know I got myself into this mess just by coming up here with Devyn. Please, Lord, don't let me die!*

"Girl," Devyn yelled. "Quit being stupid! Give me the gun. I ain't gonna ask you no more, Aisha! Give me the gun. Now!"

She turned, removing the barrel from my temple and pointed the gun at him. "You want it? Here!"

A deafening explosion ripped through the room. I screamed, horror coursing through my veins. Devyn stood, staring at Aisha with wide eyes. He turned and stared at the jagged hole in the wall behind him.

I wondered if she was simply trying to scare him or if she was just a bad shot.

"Why, you crazy—" Devyn charged toward Aisha. She kept the gun aimed at him, but her hands quivered. She looked too scared to move.

Devyn took advantage of her uncertainty and tackled her. The gun flew across the floor. While the two of them scurried, trying to reach it, I stood frozen.

Finally shaking myself out of the panic, I ran toward the front door, slipping on my shoes as I went. Just as I opened the door, I heard another shot. I stopped, my hand still on the doorknob, wondering what sound I would hear next. My heart raced as I held my breath.

Silence filled the apartment for what seemed like an eternity before I heard Devyn's voice.

"Zoe, are you still there?"

I sighed, relieved. "I'm here, Dev."

"Call the paramedics! She's been shot in the stomach. Zoe, please, call for help!"

I looked around the living room and rushed to the phone. I dialed 911 and screamed all the information to the operator. Still on the line, I opened the front door, then ran back to the bedroom.

My stomach churned at the sight that met my eyes. Blood was splattered over the carpet, the bed, the walls. It was all over Devyn's hands and clothes.

Aisha lay in his arms, holding her belly. "My baby," she squealed. "Lord, I'm sorry. Please help my baby!"

As I looked at this girl suffering in pain, then thought about that poor innocent baby who might never be born because of its mother's actions, I realized afresh the severe consequences that often follow sin. But I didn't want to spend the time judging. All I wanted to do was whatever I could to save them both.

"We need to try to stop the bleeding," I said, my voice shaking. I grabbed a pillow and threw it to Devyn. "Put this under her head," I ordered. Then I raced to the bathroom and grabbed every towel I could find.

As I returned to the room, I pushed the thought from my mind that it could have been me lying there. Or it could have been Devyn. Although this girl was definitely not out of danger, I thanked God we were all still alive.

Devyn elevated Aisha's head while I lifted her top, pulled down the waistband of her pants and pressed the towels against her gaping wound.

She looked up at Devyn with tear-filled eyes. "Do you think our baby's gonna be okay?"

"Our baby's gonna be fine," he replied.

I glared at Devyn. Before, he had tried to get with me and claimed Aisha's baby wasn't his. I wanted to call him on it, but I knew this wasn't the time. At least now I understood why she had gone to such desperate lengths. She was trying to protect her so-called family.

I heard paramedics holler from the front door.

"In here!" I called. They rushed in, pushed Devyn aside and immediately went to work on Aisha.

I picked up my purse, desperate to leave.

Devyn followed me into the hall. "Zoe, I . . . I don't—"

I whipped around, facing him. "Get in there and save your baby, Dev. And don't bother to call me. I'll be praying for you, but this is good-bye. For good."

"Zoe." He tried to hug me, but I escaped his embrace and walked out the door.

Two days after my mother's funeral and the Devyn–Aisha fiasco, I was back at work. I hadn't been at my desk for more than five minutes before my boss came to my cubicle.

"I'm so sorry to hear about your mother, Zoe. You know you didn't have to come back so soon."

"Thanks," I said. "But I needed to get busy catching up on everything. Besides, I want to be here."

"Well, let me know if you need anything," Mr. Ware said.

When he left my office, I leaned back in my chair. I was glad to be back in Seattle, away from everything in Miami.

I thought back over the last few days. Devyn called before I left Miami just to let me know that Aisha had delivered a baby boy. He was two months premature and was in intensive care.

He sounded happy as he told me the news, and I was actually happy for him. Devyn had always wanted a son. I hoped this little life would make him step up to the plate and take responsibility for what was his.

And it was time for me to take responsibility for my life as well. I didn't even want to think about what was going to happen next in my life. There was always something going on. I just wasn't sure what shape the next challenge would take.

I wanted to continue to look at things through God's eyes and hold on to Him for strength, like a blind man trusting his dog to lead. I was determined to learn that lesson and live it.

My thoughts were interrupted when my phone rang.

"Zoe, it's Shay."

"Hey, girl," I exclaimed, glad to hear from my friend. I had only spoken to her for a minute when I was in Miami. "I was about to call you to see if you got my note saying I was back. I didn't want to wake you. Do you want me to cook dinner tonight? I have a lot to tell you."

"Dinner? Zoe, haven't you heard about the rape?"

My breathing became erratic. The next challenge was rushing at me already. "What are you talking about?"

"It's all over the news. The police said Chase raped that cheerleader."

"What?" I nearly dropped the receiver.

"Coach Sykes is supposed to hold a press conference from your upstairs offices. What are you doin' sittin' at your desk, girl?"

I peeked over the wall of my cubicle. The rest of the staff was gone. The place was as quiet as a tomb. Now that I thought about it, I had noticed a frantic atmosphere when I came in that morning. I'd just figured, with the team doing so well, everyone was hyped about the play-offs. I never thought about the possibility of there being trouble. Especially not this kind of trouble. And not with Chase!

"Find a TV quick, girl," Shay shouted. "The reporters are talkin' to your boy, and he's sittin' in the back of a police car."

Hearing lots of sirens, I dropped the phone and ran to a window overlooking the parking lot between the offices and the stadium. Media vans were everywhere, surrounding a black-and-white cruiser with its lights flashing. Reporters wielding microphones followed the vehicle as it drove away. I couldn't see if Chase was in the car, but I hoped it wasn't him.

I rushed toward the conference room, shoving my way through a mass of television news crews. "Where have you been?" Mr. Ware asked, ushering me to a seat in the front row.

"I didn't know we were holding a press conference," I said meekly.

"I was sure someone would have told you," he said. "I'm sorry."

Our hushed conversation was interrupted by the coach clearing his throat at the podium. A dozen microphones were planted in front of him, and cameramen flashed photos every two seconds.

"I have had the chance to speak to Chase Farr," the coach began, "and we are firmly standing behind him. He has denied these allegations, and anyone who knows him will testify that he's a model human being, both on the field and off."

"This is crazy," I whispered to myself. Chase? Accused of rape? I had tried to give it to him and he turned me down. I know he would never take it from anybody. "This is a bunch of bull," I muttered.

Coach Sykes acknowledged one of the reporters, all of whom were flailing their hands in the air, trying to ask questions.

"Sir, the Storm cheerleaders have a reputation for conducting themselves with high moral standards. Do you really think this girl is lying?"

Oh, hush, I wanted to shout. *You don't even know Chase. Or that witch of a cheerleader. If you did, you'd know perfectly well which one was lying.*

"We do stress to all of our cheerleaders the importance of high ethical standards," Coach answered. "However, I do not have direct interaction with these girls. I don't know this particular young lady personally. I hope this was all simply a misunderstanding. Until we have further details, that's all I can say at this point."

Another reporter asked, "Coach Sykes, you've got a big game coming up this weekend. Is Chase Farr going to play?"

"We're hoping so," Coach answered. "We need him on the field, and I am going to do everything in my power to make sure that happens. But at this time, the most important thing is for this situation to be cleared up." He looked around the room. "One more question, and then I must get back to my team."

Several reporters fought for the privilege. Coach Sykes chose one.

"Last week the GM said you were hoping to sign Chase Farr to an extended contract, making him one of this team's franchise players. That deal allegedly had a lucrative signing bonus. Will those negotiations be tabled until it's determined whether or not you have a criminal on your hands?"

The room buzzed. The coach's voice silenced the din. "All I can say right now is that Chase Farr is an outstanding player, and our organization would be happy to have him with us for a long time. Our other players, many of whom have been here for years, are playing to a higher level now with Chase on board. This young athlete gives an incredible amount of physical talent to this team. But more important, he also gives his heart. Chase Farr really cares about his team, his teammates and this community. He has shown us all how to step up a notch and make great things happen."

I was thrilled to hear something positive being said about Chase in the midst of all this rubbish.

"It's a tragedy that such a man is accused of this heinous crime," Coach Sykes continued. "Until we have some solid evidence to the contrary, I personally am going to believe he's innocent." Coach Sykes left the podium, surrounded by insistent reporters.

I followed the reporters until they gave up chasing Coach Sykes. Then I continued to trail him down the hall. "Coach," I said.

He turned, looking exasperated. "Yes, young lady?"

"Sir, my name is Zoe Clarke. I work in the front office with publicity. I met you at the beginning of the season. I'm Chase's . . . ex-girlfriend." The word stuck in my throat.

"What can I do for you?" he asked in a weary voice.

"I've got to tell you something about Chase, sir. It's . . . private."

He crossed his arms and peered at me. I looked around to make sure we were alone, then whispered, "I can assure you Chase did not rape that girl."

"And how would you know that?"

I lowered my voice further. "Chase has never had sex. We broke up because I wanted him to be physical with me and he wouldn't go there."

Coach's head tilted. I definitely had his attention.

"Look, I don't have any financial resources to bail him out. But I know you do. That man has given his heart and soul to this team. I'm telling you, he's innocent. Please keep him out of jail."

Coach Sykes unfolded his arms. "Thank you, young lady." He placed his hands on my shoulders. "I promise we'll get Chase out of jail. I understand the prosecutor plans to make an example out of this case. So, it won't be easy."

I thanked him, shook his hand heartily, thanked him again and returned to my desk.

"I don't believe this," I grumbled to Shay, pacing in the apartment after work on Tuesday. "I've left countless messages on Chase's cell phone and at his apartment, but I've heard nothing. I know he's been out of jail"—I stopped and looked at my watch—"for at least four or five hours."

"Do you want to drive over to his apartment and see if he's there?" she asked.

I was waiting for Shay to ask. I had almost driven to Chase's apartment when I left work, but I didn't want to show up there alone. I didn't want him to think that I was tracking him down.

We jumped into my car, but as soon as we pulled through the gate of his guarded community, we saw hordes of media vans jammed in front of his house. And the media members were peering into every car that rolled past Chase's home.

"He couldn't be home," Shay observed, "or those pesky reporters wouldn't all still be here."

I nodded and turned the car around. "Where else can we check?"

"I don't know," Shay said. "Look, let's just go back to our place. We can't drive around town aimlessly looking for him."

My eyes filled with tears. I had to find Chase. I had to find out what was going on with him because no matter what, I still loved him. "Shay, my heart says he's hurting. I don't know where he is, but I just have this feeling he's in pain."

"Pull over," she said.

I didn't really know why, but I followed Shay's instructions. I pulled the car over to the curb and parked.

"Let's pray for him." We closed our eyes and Shay took my hands. "Father," Shay began, "Chase has got some serious stuff going on right now. Lord, we ask that You comfort him. Work this situation out so his name can be totally cleared. Expose this cheerleader for what she really is. I pray for Zoe's peace so she won't worry. Help her to know that You've got it all under control. All these things we ask in Jesus' name. Amen."

I opened my eyes. "Thanks, Shay," I said, sniffing. "I know you're right, and I've got to believe that God is handling this." I shook my head. "This isn't even my sin, and here I am acting all crazy. But things were going so well for Chase, and then, out of the blue, comes this huge mess. This kind of thing shouldn't be happening to him. I'm the one who deserves a big disaster."

"What are you saying, girl?" Shay argued. "You think you deserved all the bad things that have happened to you?"

"I know it sounds dumb, but—"

"Yeah, it does," Shay said strongly. "Now, I agree we do cause messes for ourselves sometimes. But God doesn't punish us for that. However, He does use circumstances to draw us closer to Him. Who knows? Maybe somehow He's gonna bring more people to Christ out of this whole situation."

Her words calmed my heart a bit. "You're a good friend, Shay. You should be concentrating only on your life and your wedding right now, and here you are driving with me all around town, helping me try to find a guy that ain't even mine."

"Well, let's leave Chase in God's hands and call it a night, okay?"

"Yeah." I turned on the ignition. "It's time for me to get us home."

For the rest of the week, I muddled through, trying to concentrate on work. But it was difficult. I hadn't heard from Chase. Even though I had left messages on every machine he possessed.

Being in the office didn't help. No one had any information—or at least no information that he or she was willing to pass along. Chase was in hiding, and there was no way I was going to find out where he was.

On Saturday, though, I was still hopeful. I stayed in bed all day, pager in one hand, cell phone in the other and my cordless phone just a few feet away.

It was incredibly frustrating not to have heard a word. I felt like my hands were tied and there was nothing I could do to help him. But I had to realize that God was there for Chase.

So, by the time Saturday evening rolled around, I decided to put my efforts elsewhere. I would help Chase by sending up as many prayers as I could on his behalf.

"This crazy nightmare of yours will end, Chase," I whispered into the air. "I know it. You just have to hold on." If I couldn't tell him directly, I hoped he could somehow hear my thoughts and feel my prayers.

I hardly slept Saturday night and was up before the sun on Sunday. Shay and I had made plans to attend the game and we got to the stadium well before the game started.

As we walked through the crowd, I heard nothing but conversation about Chase. My ears perked up to hear what the fans were saying.

"Everyone is innocent until proven guilty," one man was saying to another. "Chase Farr should be able to play until someone can prove that he raped that girl."

Another man complained, "This is football. All of that off-the-field stuff has nothing to do with playing ball."

Then I heard a woman say, "Well, if someone could commit such a crime against women, or even be accused of it, he shouldn't be able to play until the situation is cleared up. I tell you, if I see Chase Farr on the field, I will boycott the Storm for the rest of my life!"

Oh, brother! I wanted to scream. I was tired of hearing about it. And even more tired of not being able to do anything about it.

Shay and I sat in anticipation as we watched the teams run their pregame drills. I searched for Chase's number but couldn't find him.

"Are you sure Byron didn't say anything to you?" I asked Shay for at least the fiftieth time since I woke her up this morning.

She shook her head and answered patiently. "No. The team hasn't been told anything."

"Ladies and gentlemen, welcome to our stadium this first day of December. It's a great day for football. May I have your attention, please." The voice from the announcer's booth almost immediately silenced the stadium. Everyone was anxious for the news. "We'd like to announce that Chase Farr will be starting in today's game. . . ."

I wasn't sure if the announcer said anything else. The people in the stands exploded. But they weren't all cheers. When Chase ran onto the field, half of the people in the stands booed. I couldn't believe it. This guy had single-handedly led the team to a winning season. What a trip!

Ignoring the derision, Chase ran through the mist and came out lifting his hand as if to say, *Though they scorn me, yet will I trust the Lord.*

I sat on the edge of my seat as the game started. On the first drive, the fifth play, Chase caught a pass in the end zone for a touchdown. The boos turned to cheers.

But it didn't last long. The next time Chase touched the ball was horrendous. The quarterback overthrew the ball and Chase jumped high to get it. When he landed, his left foot turned on an angle, hitting the turf awkwardly. Chase fell to the ground.

I jumped from my seat, covering my mouth with my hand. I wanted to run to Chase—to make sure that he was all right.

The stadium was disconcertingly quiet. As the coach, the trainer and several team members surrounded Chase, Shay turned on her pocket radio, and I held it to my ear.

"Looks like Chase Farr has hurt more than just his leg," the announcer stated.

I tossed the radio back to Shay and ran from my seat. Shoving people out of my way, I ran to the sideline wall. When I caught a glimpse of Chase, he wasn't moving.

"Man, he may never play ball again," one of the players said.

I looked at the player in shock, then turned all of my attention to Chase. I wasn't concerned about whether he'd be able to play ball again; I prayed that he would be able to walk.

"Get up, Chase! Get up," I yelled, trying not to think about the dreadful possibilities. I ignored the people who turned toward me and stared as if I were a raving lunatic. I didn't care. There, still and helpless, lay the guy who had my heart. I knew there was only one thing to do. I thought about dropping to my knees, but instead I just closed my eyes. *Lord, You have to help him,* my heart cried.

A miracle had to be on its way, because the forecast on the field was grim and foggy.

Chapter 14

After holding my breath for what seemed like an eternity, the crowd in the dome started cheering. I looked up to the big screen to get a better view, and though Chase was still lying on the field, he was wiggling his fingers and toes.

My heart started beating again. "Thank you, Lord," I cried out loud.

I headed back to my seat, keeping my eyes on the screen as best as I could. When I sat down, Shay grabbed my hand and clutched it tightly.

"Looks like he probably blew out his knee, huh?" she said.

"Gosh, I hope not."

"I guess it's just a good thing he's alive."

"Yeah, no kidding. Who knows? Maybe God figures Chase has gone far enough in his career, and he needs a break. And not just his leg, you know what I'm sayin'?"

"Yeah, girl, I feel you."

A gurney was driven onto the field, and the rescue team worked to place Chase on the stretcher, then wheeled him off the field. The fans cheered and screamed. I cried.

"I'm sure he's okay," Shay assured me.

"I can't believe this." I bent my head to my lap.

"Hey, what's Byron doing?" Shay said.

I looked up and saw Byron signaling for Shay to come down to the field, near where I had been standing. My eyes followed her as she ran down to the field, talked with Byron for a moment, then started back toward me.

"Is Chase okay?" I asked Shay when she returned.

"I don't know, but Byron said that Chase asked if you were here, and when he heard you were, Chase asked him to bring you to the locker room right away."

I jumped up, anxious to go. "But I don't have a pass."

"Byron said the guy at the door will let you in."

"Okay," I said, half out of my mind.

I rushed up the stairs, then got on the elevator that took me to the locker room. Every part of my body was shaking when I knocked on the locker room's door.

"I'm here for Chase Farr," I told the guard. "My name is Zoe Clarke."

"Follow me, Ms. Clarke," he said as if he'd been expecting me.

He escorted me to a small room where Chase was still lying on the gurney. When the trainer saw me, he patted Chase's arm, nodded, then left us alone.

I stood there for a moment and stared at him. Then his tears came. I had seen Chase cry only one other time. He was always confident, rarely distressed. At that moment, he seemed like a lost child. How I wished I could remove his pain.

"It's okay," I uttered, then I kissed his forehead.

"This is crazy," he said. "I know God is trying to tell me something, but I must not be getting it."

"I don't think that's what it is, Chase," I said, taking his hand gently.

"I was just told before the game that I would be going to the Pro Bowl."

"That's great," I said, wiping his tears with my fingertips.

"No, it's not. I might not be able to play out the rest of the season."

"Until you know the extent of the damage, you shouldn't speculate."

He reached up and put his arm around my neck, pulling me closer. He kissed my lips, then said softly, "Thanks for being here."

I nodded, unable to speak after his kiss.

"I'm sorry I haven't called you," he continued. "With everything that's been going on, I haven't been the happiest guy in the world, and I needed the time alone. But I did get your messages, and I appreciate your prayers." His eyes scanned my face. "I miss you like this."

I frowned, not understanding what he was saying. "Like what?"

"By my side. I miss having you by my side."

I smiled and felt my heart warm. I was so happy to be by his side. It was an answer to every prayer.

The trainer returned. "Sorry, but we need to get him to the hospital to do some tests."

"Of course," I said, backing away.

The trainer secured the straps on the gurney and then wheeled Chase to a waiting ambulance. I followed, and then tried to get into the vehicle with him.

"Sorry, miss," the driver said, starting to shut the doors.

"No," Chase protested through the nearly closed doors. "She's got to come with me."

The driver looked from me to Chase, then shrugged. "Go ahead."

I smiled gratefully and climbed into the back. Within seconds, the ambulance took off.

I looked down at Chase. Though he tried to smile, his face revealed the terrible pain that had to be pulsating through his body. I wanted to take it away, make it all better for him, make it not hurt so bad.

But I wasn't God. I could only hope and pray that the sun would shine again for him soon.

"You know, the battle's not mine," he mumbled.

I glanced at the paramedic seated next to me, then back at Chase.

"What?" I asked.

"I said the battle's not mine. My life is crazy right now. I got that girl pressin' charges against me. My knee's blown out. I might not be asked back to the team. And I've let one of the most important things in my life slip through my fingers."

"Don't worry about that," I said, wondering which thing he meant.

"Maybe that's why I planted my foot the wrong way. In my mind, I was trippin' off stuff going on in my life instead of focusing on the game and letting God work everything else out."

"Chase, you don't have to talk about this now."

He continued as if he hadn't heard me. "It's not my battle. It's His. And there's nothin' He can't fix. God can do anything," he said as if he were trying to convince me . . . and himself. "But His ability to work in my life decreases when I take the focus off the fact that He is God."

I wasn't sure whether or not Chase realized it, but in this moment of his great pain and need, he was encouraging me.

Everything happened quickly when the ambulance pulled up to the hospital. Before I knew it, Chase had been wheeled in, and I was left in the waiting room, where I sat like a zombie.

After more than twenty minutes, a nurse came into the waiting room.

"Are you Zoe Clarke?"

I nodded.

"You can go back there now." She pointed toward the double doors, but I was through them before the nurse had even finished her sentence.

I rushed to the first section, where Chase lay on a single bed. I took his hand.

He smiled at me but remained silent.

A moment later, a white-coated doctor, with glasses halfway down the bridge of his nose, walked in with papers attached to a clipboard.

"Hello," he said through unsmiling, tight lips.

I held my breath as I anticipated his next words: *I have bad news.*

"Well, Mr. Farr," the doctor began. "It looks like you tore your PCL."

My eyes moved from the doctor to Chase, not really understanding what the doctor meant.

I breathed when I saw that Chase seemed relieved.

"What does that mean, Doctor?" I asked, turning back to the doctor.

"It's relatively good news," he explained. "You see, an ACL tear—"

I cut him off and said, "What?"

"Sorry. An Anterior Cruciate ligament tear would have meant that the main ligament in the knee was separated. That ligament doesn't grow back naturally, so surgery would be the only way to repair it. But Chase has a Post Cruciate ligament tear. That ligament is in the back of the knee, and it usually repairs itself naturally. It takes about six weeks to heal, as opposed to a year or longer."

I calculated it all in my head. Chase would be out of the play-offs. But if his team made it to the Super Bowl, he could be ready to play.

"Thank God," Chase said. Then he turned to the doctor. "Thank you."

The doctor nodded and finally smiled. "Now, it's going to take some work, and if you stay off your leg and do what I say, I think you'll be fine."

Chase nodded.

"I'll be right back."

When we were alone, Chase squeezed my hand. "Thank you too, Zoe."

I smiled as my body warmed to his words. "You don't have to thank me. I'm just glad that you're going to be fine."

The doctor and one of the team's trainers returned to the room and I backed into the corner, letting them have space to instruct Chase on what he had to do to heal.

As they talked, I talked to God. I thanked Him for His goodness and mercy and for sparing Chase. And I thanked Him for bringing Chase back into my life. I didn't know what this meant—I didn't know where this would lead. I didn't care. I just wanted to enjoy where Chase and I were right now.

The trainer drove us to Chase's apartment through a rain shower that began while we were in the hospital.

"What happened in the game?" Chase asked.

The man hesitated. "Storm lost. By six points."

Chase groaned and slumped down in the front seat.

From the back, I looked out the window and wondered if the Storm would be able to win any games without Chase. The play-off race was close. This was a bad time for Chase to be out.

The trainer helped Chase into the apartment, and I fumbled through the familiar rooms, trying to find where Chase had placed things so I could get him settled.

After the trainer left, I helped Chase into the bed, and as he lay down, I was reminded of what had separated us in the first place. I placed a pillow under his leg to prop it up, then opened the drapes for a little light.

My mind rambled back to a similar encounter. I remembered my mom entertaining Mr. Donaldson. He owned the corner liquor store and was married.

One night, somebody robbed him and beat him up. It wasn't his wife who nursed him back to health either. It was my mama. She loved on that man all night. I watched through the peephole and fell asleep there. The routine of watching her was far more damaging than any R-rated movie could ever have been. Of course I didn't know it then. When Mr. Donaldson left the next morning, he tripped over me. After apologizing and then scolding me for looking, he told me not to tell nobody he was there. He took my frail hand and placed three $100 bills in it. "This ain't yours. Go give that to yo mama and tell her thanks."

My mom did a lot for me. My soul had to forgive her because she gave so much for me.

"Looks like it stopped raining," I said, sitting on the edge of the bed, smiling as I came out of my daze.

"Yeah, but it's still drizzling," he muttered. "Just like my life." He took a deep breath and grasped my hand. "I know it's only been a few weeks, but I want to catch up. What's been going on with you?"

"Well," I began with a sigh. "Things have been kind of rough for me too." My mind filled with images of my mother, and I wished I could call my mom right now and talk to her. How many chances had I missed to do that when she was alive? Now, when I wanted to, she was gone.

Chase squeezed my fingers, interrupting my thoughts. "Please tell me about it."

"Well, my mother . . ." I lowered my head, fighting back the tears. "She . . . She passed away."

"I'm so sorry," he said, tightening his grip on my hand.

"She's had cancer for a while, but the day before Thanksgiving, my brother called me. She passed away Thanksgiving night." With watery eyes, I looked up at him. "I'm surprised that Shay didn't tell you."

He shook his head.

"I guess she was just honoring my wishes. I didn't . . . After what happened, I didn't want to bother you."

"Oh, Zoe, I wish I could have been there for you." He pulled me close to him, and I found comfort in his strong arms. For the first time in weeks, I felt safe and secure.

As I lay in Chase's arms, we talked, and we talked for hours. I told Chase about the plane that nearly crashed and the dramatic night when Aisha held a gun to my head, though I left out the part about being alone in Devyn's bedroom. I didn't want to be dishonest with Chase, but I didn't want him to take it the wrong way.

He squeezed me tighter as I talked, as if he realized how many times he could have lost me.

We were sitting totally in the dark when I realized how much time had passed. The last thing on earth I wanted to do was leave this man's side. But I knew I didn't dare stay.

"It's getting late," I said, sitting up. "I'd better get going."

"I wish you didn't have to."

Inside, I longed to climb into bed with this man, rub him all night long and make him feel so good he wouldn't ever want to let me go. But I had grown a lot in the past weeks, and although the voice of desire still spoke to me, I was able to control my passion, thanks to the One who gave me strength.

"I wish I didn't have to go too," I said, then stood. "But I do." I softly kissed his forehead. "Call me if you need anything." Then I turned around and went home.

The following Saturday, I gave Shay a wedding shower. It was easy to organize, even though I had only been back in town for a short while. Most of the wives and girlfriends of the team members attended.

"You're amazing, Zoe," Mrs. Spalding said, sipping a glass of punch. "Wherever did you come up with the idea of having the party in a bridal boutique?"

"Well, when I was helping Shay pick out her dress, she kept talking about how beautiful this store was. And the more she talked about it, the more the idea came to mind. I thought it would be special and unique."

"How did you convince the store manager to close shop on a Saturday?" Mrs. Simmons asked.

I grinned. "I told him we'd take some publicity shots of the wives and girlfriends of the Storm players trying on dresses, and mention the location in the article."

The women laughed, and it was a chuckle of admiration.

"You are a publicity genius," Mrs. Simmons said.

"The caterer and the decorator did an incredible job," Mrs. Peterson said. "You must have spent a fortune."

I chuckled. Most of the flowers and the food were donated by suppliers I'd worked with. But I didn't reveal that little tidbit. "I wanted this to be special for Shay."

The ladies exchanged glances, and I knew they were still wondering how I was paying for the affair.

Before we ate, the saleswomen helped all the women, married and single, try on the wedding gowns. And the boutique filled with laughter that mixed with the oohs and aahs. I watched to make sure that everyone had a great time, till I noticed Fawn sitting alone in a corner.

She and I hadn't talked much since we'd had that discussion about my living with Chase. I still thought that she was judgmental and critical. And I was sure she still considered me headstrong and probably a little trampy. All I wanted to do was avoid her, and so far, that had been easy.

But seeing her sitting alone, looking so dejected when everyone else was having a good time, I knew I couldn't avoid her any longer.

I took a deep breath and walked toward her, even though there was a risk that Fawn could either tell me off or tear me down. Still, I went over and sat beside her.

"Are you okay?"

She surprised me when she replied in a tearful voice: "My marriage is in trouble."

One of the ladies sauntered over to us. "What do you think, Zoe? Doesn't this dress look fabulous on me?"

"Yeah," I said. "You should definitely show that to Shay."

"Great idea," she squealed, then took off.

"Let's go someplace we can talk," I suggested to Fawn. I took her hand and led her to the back of the store.

When we were alone, Fawn's tears seemed to come faster.

"What's going on?" I asked.

She dabbed her eyes with a tissue. "First of all, I owe you an apology. I should never have accused you of pushing your boyfriend. That was really between you and Chase, and I'm sorry if I overstepped any boundaries."

"That's okay," I said. "You don't have to apologize."

"But I do. I had no right throwing stones at you. I should have been getting myself right instead. In a way, I was doing the same thing to my man."

"Well, if you want to talk, I'm here," I said. "I promise I won't judge you."

"I've wanted a baby for so long," she immediately spilled out, sounding as if she had been holding it in for such a long time. "Frankie and I have been married for five years, and I've had to watch so many other women get pregnant. It's been hard when I've wanted to be a mom so badly."

"There's nothing wrong with that," I said.

"But Frankie doesn't feel the same way. He's afraid a baby will interfere with his career."

"Oh," I said, simply understanding the picture.

"From the beginning, Frank has insisted that I take birth control pills. But a few months ago, I stopped taking them and started taking prenatal vitamins instead."

"It wasn't a joint decision," I said, making more of a statement than asking a question.

She shook her head.

"Seems to me you need to talk to your husband about this. I'm sure if you told him how much you want a child, he'd understand."

"I already tried that." She sniffed. "We've talked for more hours than I could ever count. Remember, this has been going on for five years."

"Then maybe you ought to start taking the pills again until Frank's ready."

Fawn shredded a tissue between her fingers. "That would be an easy solution . . . if I wasn't pregnant."

"You're pregnant?" I repeated her words in a whisper.

"Yeah." She began to sob again. "When Frankie finds out, he's going to be so upset . . . that I did this to him."

I couldn't believe what I was hearing. I had so many mixed feelings, but I didn't want to give her my opinion. Inside, I prayed and asked God to help me speak His words and not mine.

"A baby should be a blessing, Zoe. But I've made a big mess of everything."

"Don't talk like that," I said, even though I kinda had to agree with her. I didn't want to lecture her, the way she had lectured me. I just wanted to be her friend. "Even when we mess up," I began, "God still gives us grace. Even though you drove yourself into this crisis, I believe you can still make things right."

"How?"

"I've learned the hard way that the only way peace can happen in a relationship is through total honesty. Fawn, you have to tell your husband the truth. It might be tough, but it's really the best thing."

I hugged her. "Would you mind if we prayed together?"

It was the first time Fawn smiled. She shook her head.

I prayed with words that I knew came from God. "Father, we come to You first with praise and thanksgiving for being who You are. We ask, Father, that You give Fawn the strength that she needs to talk to her husband about this baby. Father, we know that all life comes from You, so this baby is a good thing in Your eyes. Help Frank and Fawn to see this baby the same way—the way You see the baby. In Jesus' name, Amen."

She looked up at me. Her eyes were still filled with tears, though she also wore a smile. "Thanks, Zoe. I think I can rejoin the party now."

As I walked Fawn back to the front of the store, I realized that I needed to take my own advice. "The only way peace can happen in a relationship is through total honesty."

That's what I told Fawn, and now I had to do the same

thing. I needed to tell Chase everything that was going on with me. And I needed to ask him some tough questions about Waverly too.

I glanced at Shay. She was beaming with joy. I knew that was what I wanted for myself someday.

I decided that I would talk to Chase the very first chance I got.

In the newspapers and on the news, the Storm players bragged that they were going to do fine without Chase. But they lost the next two games by more than twenty points. Chase watched the games from the sidelines and acted tough when he talked to me about the results.

"We're still the Storm," he stated with what I thought was false confidence. "The guys just have to get used to a few new plays."

I knew the losses were really bothering him.

At work, I spent my time preparing for the Storm's Christmas ball and trying to ignore the whispers I heard in the front office about Chase's case. The team's management, as well as their lawyers, seemed confident and were working diligently on clearing Chase's name. I only prayed that it would all be over soon.

Chase spent his time between home and the gym in the team's building, working on his rehabilitation. I drove him back and forth whenever I could, enjoying our time together.

Every night, I prepared dinner for him, and we spent the time talking and getting to know one another once again. I was focused on building a strong, Christ-centered relationship with Chase. Though I still had deep feelings for him, it felt great that he was finally my brother in Christ. Before I went home each night, we read the Word and prayed together. We reminded each other that God's plan was going to prevail in everything that we were going through. The spiritual relationship we were developing was even more awesome than any romantic one I could have imagined.

Still, there were things that Chase and I needed to discuss. Though I believed in my gut that he was innocent, I hadn't asked Chase about what happened with him and Waverly. And I hadn't revealed to him what happened with Devyn.

On a Friday night, I decided it was time to be completely open with Chase. We had been building our relationship on a spiritual foundation for several weeks, and I believed it could stand up to me telling him the facts about what happened with Devyn, and asking him about what happened between him and Waverly.

After I dropped Chase back home from his rehab session, I ran to the Chinese restaurant for take-out dinners. When I returned, he was sitting on the couch with a grim look on his face.

"Are you all right?" I asked. "Is your knee bothering you?"

"Yeah," he mumbled, and followed me into the kitchen.

I pulled out the food cartons and set the plates, glasses and forks on the table. I watched Chase as I worked, but he didn't look at me. He just stared silently into space.

"What's wrong?" I asked, finally sitting down. I couldn't imagine what could have happened in the twenty minutes that I'd been gone. Then it hit me. "Did something happen with your case?"

He grimaced.

"That's it, isn't it?" I reached out and touched his hand. "Chase, I've never come out and asked you, but I have to know. What went on between you and Waverly? Did you . . . do something with her?"

He glared at me and I had to sit back. He'd never looked at me that way. Obviously I had asked the wrong question.

"Well, if that's not it, what is it?" I asked, totally at a loss.

Chase continued to stare silently. I felt as if he were looking through me.

"Chase, come on. You're scaring me. Please talk to me."

I heard a noise from the back, coming from one of the bedrooms. I looked up and almost fell out of my chair. Standing in the doorway was none other than Devyn Jackson.

I sat stunned, not even moving when he sauntered over to me and planted a big, wet kiss on my lips.

"Ugh!" I said, pulling away. "What do you think you're doing?"

"Oh, come on, baby. Why you gotta treat me like that? I been tryin' to get in touch with you for nearly a month."

I could almost see the steam coming from Chase's ears. In a way, I was pleased that he was jealous, but I didn't want him to believe the bull that Devyn was talking.

"What are you doing here, Devyn?"

He grabbed a fork and the box of orange chicken and poked around in it as if he'd been invited to join us.

"Just had a little time off for the holidays," he said, talking with his mouth full. "Came to go to your last game on Sunday. Plus, check on my boy here, maybe borrow a couple of dollars and hook back up with you." He glanced at Chase. "Unfortunately, my brother here wouldn't give me no digits."

"And why do you think that was?" I asked.

"Oh, see, why you gotta be like that? Last time I saw you, we were about to go all the way, and now you talkin' like we're not together."

I couldn't believe he said that. I glanced at Chase, and his glare hadn't changed. I had to let him know what was really going on, but I didn't know what to say or do.

So, I did what I always did now when I found myself in a tough spot. I prayed. *Lord, please help me here. I know I never should have been with Devyn. I almost lost my life because of it. But please don't let me lose what I'm building with Chase.*

From inside, I got the courage to say, "Look, Devyn, when I left you and Aisha, y'all were having your baby. She was crazy, trying to kill us, but you were still there for her. I don't know what's going on between you two, but I'm not the girl for you. And you are definitely not the guy for me!"

"Yeah, well, that's not what your body was sayin' when you were rubbin' up against me a few weeks ago."

Chase's expression changed. Gone was the glare, replaced by sadness. Devyn's words were hurting him, and I wished to God that I could deny what was being said. But I knew I had to be honest.

"So sue me; I'm human," I said, trying to be real. "Sure, I wanted the physical love of a man that night. I had just buried my mother. But once I was in your arms, I knew that I couldn't settle for you. All the time that your arms were around me, I was really needing Chase." Though I continued to speak to Devyn, I turned to Chase. "I realized the only man I wanted was Chase. I wanted him."

"What?" Devyn said, sticking the fork into the box of chicken and tossing it back on the table. "You talkin' about *this* brotha'? The one that's got a white girl suing him 'cause he had to take it from her?"

Chase stood, and I was sure he was ready to punch Devyn in the face. I jumped between them.

"No, guys. Please don't do this." I pointed at Devyn. "Devyn, I don't know why you came all the way here to start this mess. I thought we left that stuff settled back in Miami. Chase doesn't want me like that, okay? We're just friends." I looked at Chase, and when he said nothing, my heart dropped. I turned back to Devyn. "I hope that makes you feel better." I rushed out the door.

Rain poured from the sky as I stood in the parking lot, fighting my feelings of frustration. I pointed my face into the wind, not caring a bit about getting wet.

I finally locked myself inside my car. "I get myself into more messes! Now that I know who I really want to be with, it looks like it's too late. I've done so much damage to Chase, I'm sure I've pushed him away forever. Lord, I need Your help. I'm really sick of the hard times. Even though this isn't a full-blown disaster, it is a lot all at once. I need help in this deluge!"

Chapter 15

For the next few days, during which the team lost its last game, I didn't see or speak to Chase. I waited for him to call me, but when he didn't, I decided to give him his space. I knew there was serious damage this time to our relationship. First I'd asked him if something had happened with Waverly, and then Devyn . . . I feared that things might never be the same.

But I couldn't focus on that. I'd had a lot to do with only days before the Christmas charity ball for the Seattle Storm. It had turned into a charity event, at $500 a ticket, benefiting the children's home that Chase and I had visited. It was Chase's suggestion to give the home new computers, beds and clothing for the children.

Finally, Christmas Eve arrived and I was nervous and ecstatic at the same time. The Swiss Hotel ballroom looked magical, like a fairy castle straight out of "Cinderella."

The kids from the home were invited to attend for free. I'd convinced the owner of a local department store to donate clothes for the children to wear, and they looked like angels.

The owner had asked the team even in defeat to attend the charity event. They weren't going to the play-offs, but they could sure give something back to the community. I knew Chase felt bad, unable to contribute due to his injury. Certainly the team realized now what a big asset he was.

I spent the evening bustling from one place to another, making sure everything was happening the way it was supposed to. As I hustled between the kitchen and the buffet table, Shay stopped me.

"Hey, girl. You look great. That dress is beautiful."

I glanced at my cream knit gown and smiled. "Thanks, girl." We hugged. "You look stunning too, girlfriend," I said, admiring her red-and-black satin gown.

"I've been looking all over for you," she said, lowering her voice.

"Why? What's up?"

"Aren't you excited about the charges being dropped against Chase?"

"Are you serious?" I asked, grabbing Shay's shoulders. I couldn't believe I hadn't heard, even though I had spent most of the day at this hotel getting ready for tonight. "What happened?"

She frowned. "You didn't know?"

I shook my head and repeated, "What happened?"

"Well, Byron just told me the charges were dropped after some of the Storm cheerleaders said Waverly told them the real story." Shay lowered her voice even more. "Apparently she wanted to sleep with Chase so she could get pregnant and he'd marry her. When he wouldn't get with her, she made this claim. She never wanted it to go so far as a public rape charge, but things got out of hand."

"Out of hand?" I exclaimed. "That's an understatement. Are they pressing charges against her for making false accusations?"

Shay nodded. "I think so. I know she's not a cheerleader anymore."

"Good." I didn't want to wish bad things on anyone, but this girl had almost ruined Chase's reputation and life with her craziness.

"I can't believe you didn't know this. I thought Chase would have filled you in."

I shook my head. "We had kind of an . . . argument, a blow up. . . . I don't know what you would call it."

"Really?" Shay's eyes widened.

"The other day." I thought back to the way Chase had looked at me when Devyn said all those things. "It's over between us, Shay. I'm sure I've lost him for good this time."

From the corner of my eye, I saw Fawn waving to get my attention. "Can you excuse me for a minute?"

"Yeah, no problem," Shay said. "I gotta go check on my man anyway." She hugged me. "Don't worry about Chase, girl. He's gonna be okay. And I have a feeling the two of you will be all right too."

I shrugged. I wasn't going to argue with her and tell her there was slim chance of that.

I rushed over to Fawn. She hugged me tight. "I told Frankie everything, Zoe, just like you said. I prayed a lot, and then I was completely honest with him."

"How'd he react?"

She looked at me with dancing eyes. "He was totally

understanding. He said he's ready to be a daddy, and he's happy and excited."

"Oh, Fawn, that's fantastic!" I hugged her again. "God is so awesome."

She dabbed at the corner of her eye, trying not to ruin her makeup. "I can't thank you enough for encouraging me to be up front and truthful. My life's at a much better place now. You're a great friend, Zoe Clarke."

"Hey, I didn't do anything."

She lowered her eyes. "You did a lot. After the way I talked to you about Chase, I wouldn't have blamed you if you'd never spoken to me again. But you didn't turn your back on me. You took the time to get involved with what was happening to me."

"Fawn." I tilted my head to get her to look back up at me. "You were right all along . . . about me and Chase. I didn't see it at the time. But if I had taken your advice, maybe I wouldn't have lost Chase totally. Maybe none of the terrible things that have happened to both of us would have occurred. You confronted me in love, and that's what the Bible tells us to do. So, I understand what you said to me."

She smiled and nodded as if she were grateful for my words. "The Word also says we're to bear one another's burdens and lift up fellow believers. Like you did."

"I'm just glad I could be there for you," I said, squeezing her hand. "Hey, you know what?"

"What?"

"Y'all are gonna have a baby!"

She smiled. "You're right. I'm going to be a mommy."

"You're having a baby?" Shay asked Fawn, coming up behind me.

"Yes, Shay. I am." Fawn looked radiant, glowing like a new mother already.

"That is so wonderful! Congratulations." Shay embraced Fawn carefully, like she was a fragile china doll.

"Well," Shay said. "I'm going to head over to the chapel now."

"I still can't believe you're getting married at midnight tonight," Fawn said.

"Well, my parents got married at midnight on Christmas Eve, and so did my grandparents. And they're all still married."

"It's not easy to make a marriage last these days," Fawn said. "Especially when you're married to a professional football player."

"Have you heard about Dre Simmons and his wife?" Shay whispered.

"What about them?" I asked.

"I heard she caught him cheating with a fan," Fawn said.

"Yeah," Shay confirmed. "Byron told me it's hard to resist all those gorgeous girls just waiting outside the stadium after every game, giving out their numbers . . . and other things."

"It's even more difficult when the team goes to away games," Fawn added. "You're out there in a strange city, lonely, without the one you love. Somebody comes up to you, looking all fine, offering you a good time. A woman hands you a piece of paper with her phone number on it. You go back to your empty hotel room, and there's that number, just sitting there calling to you."

"Hey," I argued, "it's not like they have to take it in the first place."

"That's true," Fawn agreed.

"Well, I really don't want to talk about this right now. That ain't gonna happen to Byron and me. I know he's gonna be faithful," she said seriously, and then added with a mischievous grin, "If he ever cheats on me, I'll mess him up so bad he'll wish he'd been tackled by a four-hundred-pound linebacker!"

We laughed. I could just imagine sweet little Shay beating up her man!

"Hey, y'all," Shay said. "Make sure you get to the chapel on time."

"Don't worry," I said. "This should be over about ten, and the chapel's right up the street."

"You'd better be there," Shay said. "I ain't walkin' down that aisle without you two!"

"And don't worry about Byron either," Fawn said. "I'll be sure he gets there too." She looked around. "By the way, have you seen him?"

"My husband-to-be is playing with some of the kids, God bless him."

I looked at Shay, who was watching her man with a sold-out look in her eyes. I felt a twinge of jealousy, but it passed quickly. My wedding day had been ruined, but it never should have happened in the first place. And I knew my time would come, when God knew it was right.

"Girl," I said to Shay. "You've been waiting a long time to be with that brother. You gonna be able to handle him?"

"Oh, yeah," she sighed. "You know it." She wandered toward Byron and the kids. I watched her, longing for the day when I'd have the kind of relationship she had with Byron.

"Are you all right?" Fawn asked softly.

I hadn't meant to feel sorry for myself, but I guess the sadness showed on my face.

"Don't worry, girl. Your time is coming," she assured me.

"I know," I said. "But, Fawn, I'm not pure like Shay. My dress is gonna have to be cream instead of white."

Fawn put her arm around me. "That won't matter because of where your heart is now. That's all God asks us to do—that when we know better, we do better. And when God puts you with the man that He's chosen for you, you'll be able to wear a dress as pure and as white as new snow."

I couldn't speak as tears came to my eyes.

"Excuse me, Ms. Clarke." I turned to one of the waiters holding an empty tray.

Immediately switching to my business side, I swallowed my sorrow. "Is there a problem?"

He looked around to make sure he wouldn't be overheard. "We seem to be out of pumpkin pie."

"That's impossible," I said. "Excuse me, Fawn. I've got to take care of something. I'll catch up with you later, okay?"

"No problem," Fawn said.

I led the waiter to the manager, and the matter got cleared up immediately. The hotel didn't want to lose the business of the Storm. When the fire was put out, and dessert was served, I returned to the gala. I saw Fawn and Shay talking in a corner, smiling and laughing. Honestly, my heart was happy for both of them. The bond between us had really grown. We were three very different women, but we had some important things in common. We all had a deep love for Christ and an appreciation for one another. And we were determined to be there for each other. Those things made for a special friendship. I didn't do so well with my friendships back in Miami. But now that God had given me another chance in that area, I wasn't gonna blow it.

My eyes fixed on the most handsome man in the room. Chase Farr stood a few feet away from my girlfriends. It wasn't the first time I'd seen him, but it felt that way. Love at first sight. I was mesmerized when he first walked into the room, looking so good in his black tuxedo with satin lapels. It seemed he wasn't my man anymore, but he was still near and dear to my heart.

A crowd of television and newspaper reporters surrounded him, all asking questions at the same time. I wondered why they were so into him, since the charges had been dropped.

"We want details, Mr. Farr," one persistent reporter was saying. "What numbers are on that contract you signed?"

Contract? I wondered.

Coach Sykes intervened. "After we lost those last games, I knew I needed to sign this man right away." He clapped Chase on the back. "Besides his skills on the field, he's a good guy too. As soon as we received word that the case was dropped and he was cleared of all the charges, we offered him the best deal we could."

The reporters clamored for details.

Coach held up his hand and waited for the din to subside. "I am happy to announce that Chase Farr has signed a four-year contract with a twelve-million-dollar signing bonus. This guy'll be pulling down around forty-two mill altogether."

I could have choked. Not that I didn't believe Chase

deserved it, but I remembered when just a few months before, none of this seemed possible. I wanted to run up and congratulate him. But instead, I wished Chase well in my heart and went back to doing my job and making sure the night was a success.

That night we raised $150,000 for the children's home. More than enough for every kid to get all the things they'd asked Santa for, and then some!

Although the ball was supposed to end at nine o'clock, it was after ten P.M. by the time all of the guests were gone. Still, I had final details I had to finish with the hotel staff and with my boss. It was almost 11:30 P.M. when Mr. Ware looked at his watch and dismissed me.

"You did a fantastic job," he said. "Unbelievable."

"Thanks," I said.

"Now, you get yourself to that wedding, all right?" He grinned.

"Yes, sir!"

I jumped into my car and headed up the street to the chapel. When I walked into the small, quaint building, I stopped, smiling at the glow of candlelight. There had to be at least one hundred candles flickering everywhere. Even without all the guests, the room was filled with joy and love.

This was what a special day was all about. Shay had saved herself for a godly man. Although her groom wasn't as pure as she was, he had rededicated himself to the Lord and honored their sacred union. And he had never pressured her to give in sexually.

I wanted to stand in the midst of this feeling, but I knew

Shay needed me. I raced to the bride's room, where Shay was already dressed and looking gorgeous. Fawn looked beautiful too, in the tea-length peach gown Shay had chosen for her bridesmaids to wear.

I sighed as I stared at my friends.

"Now, don't start crying," Shay warned. "I have a feeling things are gonna turn around for you. Maybe sooner than you think."

I nodded, and turned away from Shay. I had to get myself under control. The tears I felt building behind my eyes were for more than Shay. Yes, they were for her joy, but they mixed with the sorrow I felt for myself.

Fawn helped me get ready, and then we took our positions at the doorway.

I turned to Shay and kissed her cheek. "I am so happy for you, girl. You deserve the best. Just know that I love you, and I wish you all of God's blessings today and for the rest of your life."

Though her lips trembled, she smiled. "Thank you, Zoe."

At the sound of the music cue, Byron's brother took Fawn's arm and led her down the aisle. Shay's brother escorted me a few steps behind. After we separated at the bottom of the altar and took our places, the music paused.

When the wedding march began, the congregation stood. Shay walked down the aisle, on her father's arm, looking like a princess from a storybook.

As Shay and Byron said their vows, I knew heaven was smiling down on them. Nothing but good things were going to come from this union.

Though I worked to keep my eyes focused on the couple,

I tried to find Chase in the crowd. I just wanted to look at him, smile at him. But he was nowhere in sight.

I frowned. I couldn't believe that Chase would miss Byron's big day. And then as I thought about it, I felt bad. Chase probably didn't come because he didn't want to see me.

I turned back to the couple and planted my bridesmaid smile back on. After my best friend and her man were proclaimed husband and wife, the guests adjourned to the fellowship hall, while we took photos. While I was able to smile and pose, my eyes still searched for Chase. After a while, I realized he just wasn't going to show up.

I was glad when the photographer released us; my cheeks were hurting from smiling. We joined the guests, where we were all served hors d'oeuvres, a sparkling apple cider toast and banana-crème-filled wedding cake.

When I glanced through the windows, I noticed that it was raining again—so typical for Seattle—but that didn't dampen the occasion.

At two in the morning, Shay found me sitting at a corner table, rubbing my feet and trying desperately to keep my eyes open.

"Zoe," she said, her face flushed with excitement, "I know you're exhausted, but could I ask you for one more favor?"

"Sure," I said, secretly hoping it wouldn't take more than ten minutes, because that was about how much longer I thought I could stay awake.

"Would you drive us to the cruise ship?"

"What?" I cried. "Now?" I was excited as anyone that the soon-to-be Mr. and Mrs. Johnson were going to be taking a cruise to Alaska for their honeymoon, but I couldn't believe that she wanted me to take her to the ship in the middle of the night.

"It would really mean a lot to me."

"First of all, who's going to let you on the boat at this time of night? It's not sailing until tomorrow."

Shay grinned. "You forget that I'm married to an NFL player. Special provisions were made."

"Okay, but don't you guys have mothers or aunts or uncles or anyone who can do that for you?" I hoped I didn't sound cranky, but I was completely worn out. Why hadn't she taken care of this before the wedding? Every other detail was planned.

"Please," she begged when she saw my hesitation. "It would mean a lot to both of us."

I looked into her exuberant face. How could I turn down the simple request of a girl who meant so much to me? She needed my help, and I'd promised myself and God to focus on being there for my friends. What was one night without sleep? I could stay in bed as late as I wanted to in the morning. It was Christmas and I would be spending the day by myself anyway.

I gave Shay a weary smile.

She clapped her hands like a giddy little girl. "You're awesome, Zoe!"

"You're right about that," I pretended to brag. "And don't you forget it!"

"Don't worry," she said sincerely. "I won't."

When we reached the cruise ship, I was kinda surprised. It wasn't even half the size of the ones I'd seen in Miami.

"This is a private charter," Byron explained. "We're going to be the only passengers."

Wow! I thought. *It really does pay to marry an NFL player.*

"Come on board for a minute," Shay invited me. I groaned. "Please, you've got to see this! It's absolutely breathtaking."

I didn't feel comfortable. I felt a bit like I was invading their honeymoon. But I wanted to do this last thing for my friend before she sailed off into the moonlight.

Byron swept Shay into his arms and carried her up the metal ramp. I looked at the two large suitcases and two smaller bags sitting in the open trunk of my Probe. Not wanting to ruin their romantic moment, I piled the two smaller bags on my shoulders and got help from a crew member to roll the larger suitcases.

Shay was right. It was beautiful. White roses adorned every railing and doorway.

"Girl, your hubby sure went all out for you," I said, relieving my arms of the heavy suitcases.

"I know." She beamed as Byron set her down.

"Now, where do you want all this stuff, girl? It's heavy!"

A tall woman in a crisp white uniform approached. "Welcome aboard," she said. "Come this way." She started toward the back of the ship. Byron grabbed the two large suitcases, and I picked up the smaller ones.

The woman ushered us to a tiny room decorated with more white roses, then disappeared. As I dropped the bags onto the bed, I felt the ship moving. "Wait a minute! What's going on? I've got to get off."

"Relax," Shay said, grinning at me.

"Relax? I have to get out of here. I can't go with you on your honeymoon!" I headed for the door.

"Okay, wait right here, Zoe," Byron said. "I'll go let the captain know." Byron left the room, but not before kissing his bride.

I exhaled. That would have been a disaster—being the third wheel on a honeymoon!

Shay said, "While Byron's doing that, maybe you can help me unpack a few things."

I nodded.

Shay turned to me, her face still flushed. "Thanks so much, Zoe, for everything you've done for me."

"Yeah, whatever," I said, really feeling tired. I couldn't wait to get home and soak in a tub of hot, bubbly water.

"Listen, I have *got* to go to the bathroom. It's been hours! Wait here. I'll be right back."

When Shay left the room, I walked to the porthole and looked outside. The ship didn't seem to be stopping. It actually looked like it was picking up speed. I hoped Byron could get the captain to turn around soon.

I glanced up at the clear, star-filled sky, thinking about the past few months. It seemed like every minute I'd either been smack in the middle of a horrible problem, about to go through one or just coming out of one.

But each had taught me something. First there was Devyn, and I learned that I really had to trust that the Lord knew what was best for me. Then I thought about my mother. I really missed her, but I learned that I couldn't judge people and that life was just too short and precious to carry around old baggage. Finally, my mind drifted to Chase. It seemed that his was the biggest lesson of all. I learned that I could be my own enemy, that I could block my own blessings. "I miss you, my love," I uttered aloud.

"Who do you miss?" a soft male voice whispered. Before I could turn around, two strong arms encircled my waist.

My mouth opened wide. I reached up and touched the face behind me. It was the familiar one I'd grown to love so much.

Chase turned me around to face him. The love in his eyes told me he was feeling all the same emotions I was.

"Zoe, over the past week, since I last saw you, I've spent a lot of time with God. And everything is starting to look up for me finally. The charges were dropped. I got that great contract with the team. I know God has done all this." He lifted my chin with his index finger. "But I keep hearing Him tell me I need more. I need you." He drew me close and kissed me passionately.

Against every instinct and desire in my body, I pulled back. "What are you doing, Chase? We've been here before. We don't need to go here again."

"Zoe"—he started his speech—"I've wanted you for such a long time. You're so beautiful physically, but also spiritually. I know that in my weakest moments, you were praying for me, lifting me up before God."

I stared at him, wondering what was going on. I didn't understand anything. I didn't understand where his words were leading. I didn't understand what had happened to Shay and Byron. And I didn't understand what Chase was doing on this boat that was still moving, making its way to the sea.

"Devyn told me he tried to get back with you," Chase said through my thoughts. "But that you stopped him.

When he finally told me that, I can't tell you how I felt. I waited four years for you to want me. And now that you do, I don't want to lose you." He slowly lowered himself to one knee and pulled out a sparkling pear-shaped diamond nestled in a platinum band. "Zoe Clarke, will you be my wife?"

I gasped. Tears flowed down my cheeks like rain. Unable to speak, I nodded vigorously.

Chase stood, a huge smile on his face. He kissed me like he'd never done before. When he pulled back, I was breathless. "Now, close your eyes."

Although filled with confusion, I obeyed without question. I heard Chase open a squeaky door. Then he took my hand and said, "Okay, now open them."

When I lifted my eyelids, I found myself gazing at the most beautiful white lace gown I had ever seen. Without taking my eyes off the dress, I asked, "What's this?"

"Everything's arranged with the ship's captain. Shay and Byron are going to be our witnesses. I already got the marriage certificate. We can get married right now, if you're willing."

I stared at Chase. "Are you serious?"

"Very," he said, his face and voice sincere. "I want to love you the way you've always wanted to be loved. The way I've always wanted to love you."

"But, Chase," I said, realizing that one small but important cloud was interfering with the joy of the moment, "I can't wear that."

"Why not?" he asked, his creased forehead revealing his confusion.

"It's . . . white." I turned my head, trying not to cry. Although I remembered Fawn's earlier words, I still didn't believe that I was worthy. "I can't wear a white wedding dress."

Chase turned me around, took my chin in his fingers and gently tilted my head to face him. "Zoe, you're so wrong about that. Don't you know, you've been washed pure and clean by the blood of Jesus Christ? He forgives us for every transgression and separates us from our sins as far as the east is from the west. He knows we've both repented for our past mistakes. I made mistakes toward you too, Zoe. I should have proposed to you long ago. I shouldn't have made it my job to test you. That's only God's job. And the Bible says God remembers our past mistakes no more. If He doesn't, we shouldn't either."

I couldn't believe God had blessed me with such a perfect, wonderful man.

"So, will you marry me tonight?"

I nodded as Chase used his thumbs to wipe the tears from my cheeks.

There was a knock on the door and Shay peeked in.

"May we come in now?" she asked, a wide smile filling her face.

I hugged my friend with my tears still falling. Then Shay rushed Chase from the room.

"Get out of here," she said. "I've got to get this bride ready."

Thirty minutes later, Chase and I were standing under the covered portion of the ship's deck.

A soft mist blanketed us as the captain performed the ceremony that would make me one with Chase, the man I truly loved and who loved me. After we said, "I do," and the captain pronounced us husband and wife, Chase carried me back to the room where he had proposed.

We spent minutes kissing passionately, but it wasn't long before he gently removed the beautiful white dress from my trembling body. I really did feel like a pure, untouched bride about to be loved for the very first time.

I stopped kissing him just long enough to whisper, "I love you, my husband."

He smiled, cupping my cheeks in his hands. "I love you too, my sweet wife."

I was living in the middle of a fairy-tale moment. And to think, I thought God was blessing me months before to be with a man who had a steady job. Well, when I got right with God, He opened up the windows of heaven and poured a real blessing on me. With Chase, it looked as though we would never need to worry about providing for our future. God is awesome.

"What are you thinking?" he asked as he gently rubbed my cheek.

Standing on my toes, I kissed his forehead and said, "The team will probably fire me when they find out I'm your wife. But I guess we'll be okay, though, huh?"

Sarcastically, he joked, "Yeah, looks like we're gonna make it. Seriously, though, honey, your party was great. If you want to look at starting your own party-planning business, I'll support you."

I just hugged him. That was a great idea. Boy, did I love him. Everything was perfect—well, except Tasha wasn't in my life anymore. Being honest with myself, I missed her.

"Baby, where'd you go? What's wrong?" he asked with such concern that I had to share my thoughts.

"You know my girlfriend, Tasha; well, I just . . ." I was unable to continue; I choked up so bad.

"You love her; she was your best friend. You can and will work it out with her. It's almost the off-season. Maybe we can invite her up next year."

My husband was all that. Okay I was done with the girl-friend issues. I was ready to be his wife.

As though sensing I was totally ready, he picked me up and placed my naked body on the bed. I caressed the muscles of his back as he climbed on top of me. My hus-band made love to me slowly and easily. I had thought I'd have to teach him certain things because I was the one with the experience, but that wasn't the case at all. He held me, caressed me, made me feel good everywhere. He met my every need. Just like the pro he was on the field, he was an all-star in the bedroom. His bummed leg didn't give him a problem. God blessed our union.

I felt our holy union become one in every sense of the word. Afterward, as I lay naked in his arms, tears flowed once more from my eyes.

"Are you okay?" Chase asked, concern etched on his face.

"Very okay," I assured him. "It's amazing. I really felt like a virgin for you, and I'm so thankful. I know it's a sign from God, letting me know that I'm truly yours. You were right, my darling. The past has nothing to do with our future. I've been forgiven for that, and I feel so free."

Outside, the light rain had turned into a raging storm, lightning and thunder providing God's own music and illumination for our moment. We wanted no other sound.

We slept in each other's arms, swaying to the ocean's motion. By the time I opened my eyes, the sun had risen on a beautiful, clean morning—a symbol of the dawn of newness for Mr. and Mrs. Chase Farr. This was a blessed day that the Lord had made just for us.

"I can't believe we're married," I said to Chase the moment he opened his eyes.

"I don't deserve this," Chase echoed. "But I sure do thank the Lord for you."

As I held my new husband in my arms and looked at the beautiful view outside our window, I realized that God uses storms in our lives to refine us with His glory. So, I wasn't afraid of the raging winds or uncertainties. I knew we are never alone when the wind blows. I wasn't wishing trouble for my new life, but I believed that if drama came, Chase and I could handle it with God showing us how. It was kinda like I had a "So bring on the storm" attitude—I could handle it.

I learned that only when God was the lova' of my life did I find the happiness I longed for since my dad's death nineteen years ago. Only when I accepted Jesus Christ into my heart did I know how it felt to be completely in love. And only when I let the Holy Spirit come dwell within me was I ready to be joined in marriage to a godly man.

And if we hold on to His unchanging hand and stay rooted and grounded in Him, there will always be after the storm—like the spectacular view that filled the horizon before me—a brilliant rainbow.

About the Author

Stephanie Perry Moore is truly a woman from the South. She was born in South Carolina, raised in Virginia, educated in Alabama and resides in Georgia. She is the author of the successful Payton Skky series for teenagers. She is also the general editor of several Bible products for World Bible Publishers and Nia Publishing. She lives in the greater Atlanta area with her husband, Derrick, and their two young daughters, Sydni and Sheldyn.

Reading Group Guide

Chapter One

1. Zoe's plans for a perfect wedding were rained upon by her unfaithful fiancé, leaving her hurt and confused. When has an unexpected turn of events threatened to ruin plans you have made for your life, causing you to reassess everything you believe in? Read **Job 17:11, 42:2** and **Proverbs 19:21.**

2. Based on her prayer, Zoe recognized that being sexually active with Devyn was not in God's will, yet she continued to be sexually active before marriage. Why do human beings tend to ignore the will of God in chosen areas of their lives, yet seek His blessings in those same areas? How can we grow to trust in His plan for our lives? Read **Exodus 19:5; Proverbs 16:3; Jeremiah 7:23, 29:11.**

Chapter Two

3. Zoe was devastated when Devyn left her at the altar. After her disastrous wedding day, she had to begin picking up the pieces of her life. How can we know that the Lord is with us even as we face the darkest times of our lives? Read **Deuteronomy 31:8; Joshua 1:9; Isaiah 43:2** and **John 14:27.**

Chapter Three

4. Being jilted at the altar left Zoe feeling like her circumstances were so bad that not even the Lord could redeem them. How can people gain hope that the Lord can bring glory to Himself even through the worst of circumstances? Read **Genesis 18:14; Jeremiah 32:27; Isaiah 6:57.**

5. Chase told Zoe that he wanted God's will to be done in his life more than he wanted the desires of his heart. How can we know that our desires are within the will of God? Read **Psalms 37:4, 23, 31, 119:133; 2 Timothy 2:22.**

Chapter Four

6. Zoe blinded herself to reality regarding her relationship with Devyn. Later she acknowledged that Devyn wasn't the kind of man she needed. What happens to believers when we surrender our will and our lives to the will of God? Read **Psalms 4:5, 37:5–7; Proverbs 3:5–6.**

Chapter Five

7. For a time, it appeared as though Chase would not be a player for the Seattle Storm although it was his heart's desire to play professional football. How can believers continue to give testimony to the Lord even when it appears as though we may have lost our heart's desires? Read **Psalms 27:14, 130:5; Isaiah 40:30–31.**

Chapter Six

8. After Zoe had been wronged at the altar, even more horrible things began happening to her. How can believers know that the enemy is not winning during those times when it feels like we're being kicked when we're already down? Read **Psalms 13, 31:15–24.**

9. As Zoe and Chase continued to share the same apartment, Zoe became increasingly aware of her physical desire for him. What should Christians do to keep their hearts and minds focused on things that will not lead them astray? Read **Romans 13:13–14; 1 Corinthians 6:19; 1 Thessalonians 4:3–7.**

Chapter Seven

10. Zoe's attraction to Chase continued to escalate, especially as he excelled in his football career and began gaining the attention of fans, the media, and even other women. Furthermore, she was thrilled that he cared deeply, too. How did her actions reveal that Zoe still did not have a full appreciation for the kind of man Chase was or for the kind of relationship God desired for the two of them? Read **1 Samuel 16:7; 1 Corinthians 6:18–20.**

11. Fawn gave Zoe good advice, although it was cloaked in judgment. How can Christians share their godly wisdom and insights with God so that the message will be interpreted as loving and not judgmental? Read **Psalms 116:5; Matthew 9:36; Ephesians 4:32; Colossians 3:12.**

Chapter Eight

12. Zoe believed her living arrangements with Chase were acceptable, primarily because they were not sleeping together. They failed to consider the temptation brought on by two people in love sharing living quarters before they were married. What

are the consequences of believers ignoring the fact that they are stepping into spiritual storms and personal blizzards? Read **1 Thessalonians 5:21–24.**

Chapter Nine

13. After their argument in the motel room, Zoe wondered why the Lord would not take away her feelings of desire for Chase. In what way does Zoe's prayer indicate a lack of trust in God? What should believers do when we seem unable to trust God and control our desires and urges? Read **2 Samuel 22:26–37.**

Chapter Ten

14. In a more compassionate way, Amy was able to express Christian concern for Zoe and Chase's living arrangements. How can believers know when we are involved in activity that offers a flawed witness to the world? Read **Romans 12:1–2.**

15. Zoe's sexual advances toward Chase seemed to reveal that she only knew how to show love and compassion through sex. How can Christians appropriately demonstrate love, caring, joy and other positive feelings to others, especially members of the opposite sex? Read **Ruth 2:1–16, 3:3–13.**

16. After their breakup, Zoe began to realize that she needed a life of her own and a deeper relationship with the Lord. Why are many female believers prone to throw their energies into a intimate human relationship, rather than an intimate relationship with God? Read **Genesis 3:16b; Song of Songs 5:6–8.**

Chapter Eleven

17. Zoe's temporary breakup with Chase gave her the time and opportunity to build a closer relationship with the Lord as well as with her own mother. How can unforeseen or unfortunate circumstances help believers grow closer to the Lord and repair damaged relationships with others? Read **Psalms 73:21–28.**

18. Zoe's concern for her own problems blinded her to the fact that others were having problems, too, such as her mother. Mercifully, the Lord allowed the two of them to resolve their issues and grow closer before her mother's death. How can believers be

more sensitive to the concerns of others, even as we struggle with our own problems? What spiritual truths can we learn by being alert to the concerns of other persons? Read **Colossians 3:12–17.**

Chapter Twelve

19. Although she was hurt that Chase had begun dating someone else, Zoe recognized that the situation was the result of her own creation. How does Zoe's acceptance of the consequences of her actions reveal that she was maturing, both spiritually and emotionally? Read **Ephesians 4:11–15.**

20. Devyn reappeared when Zoe was most vulnerable to temptation. How does Satan use our vulnerability to tempt us with things or people that seem to be the solution to our problem? What can believers do to avoid getting in situations that lead them into temptation? Read **Matthew 26:41; 1 Corinthians 10:13; Colossians 3:1–5.**

Chapter Thirteen

21. How did Zoe jeopardize her future by putting herself in a dangerous situation with Devyn? Why do you think she ignored reason and went to his residence despite everything that had happened between them? Pray a prayer of thanksgiving to the Lord for His grace that has covered you, shielding you from hurt, harm, and danger. Read **Judges 16:20; Psalms 20:1, 30:2–4, 59:1, 69:30.**

22. Zoe realized the severe consequences of sin as she watched Aisha lying on the floor injured. What can people do to return to the Lord, despite the consequences of their sinfulness? Pray to the Lord for His forgiveness and mercy in the situations you have created in your life because of your sinfulness and the consequences that resulted. Read **1 Corinthians 15:31–34; Galatians 5:7–9.**

Chapter Fourteen

23. Chase attributed his accident to allowing his problems to distract him from being focused on the Lord. How are believers affected when we allow our problems or circumstances to take

our attention off of the Lord? Read **1 Chronicles 16:11; Matthew 14:25–32.**

24. When Devyn confronted Zoe, his words were hurtful to Chase, yet Zoe could not deny what he was saying. A moment of vulnerability had returned to haunt her and hurt someone she loved deeply. What does this encounter between Devyn, Zoe, and Chase reveal about the need to make careful choices every moment of the day? Read **Proverbs 8:28–30; 1 Peter 3:15–17.**

Chapter Fifteen

25. Only a few months earlier when Zoe wanted to marry Devyn she thought she was blessed to be with a not-so-faithful man with an average annual income. Through trial and struggle, the Lord brought her through to blessings beyond her imagination. Ask yourself if the Lord is pulling you through a storm in order to give you greater blessings. Pray and ask the Lord if you are in any way hindering those blessings from coming to you. Finally, pray for strength to endure the journey as you grow to receive the fullness of what the Lord has in store for you. Read **Psalms 142:7; Ephesians 3:20–21; 2 Corinthians 9:11; Philippians 4:4–9, 19.**